My HOLIDAY HOOKUP Roadtrip

A
HOT UNDER THE MISTLETOE
ROMANCE

LARGE PRINT

SARA WHITNEY

My Holiday Hookup Road Trip: Large Print Edition

Copyright © 2022 Sara Whitney

Published by LoveSpark Press

Ebook ISBN: 978-1-953565-11-2
Print ISBN: 978-1-953565-18-1
Large Print ISBN: 978-1-953565-22-8

First Edition: December 2022

v. 1.4

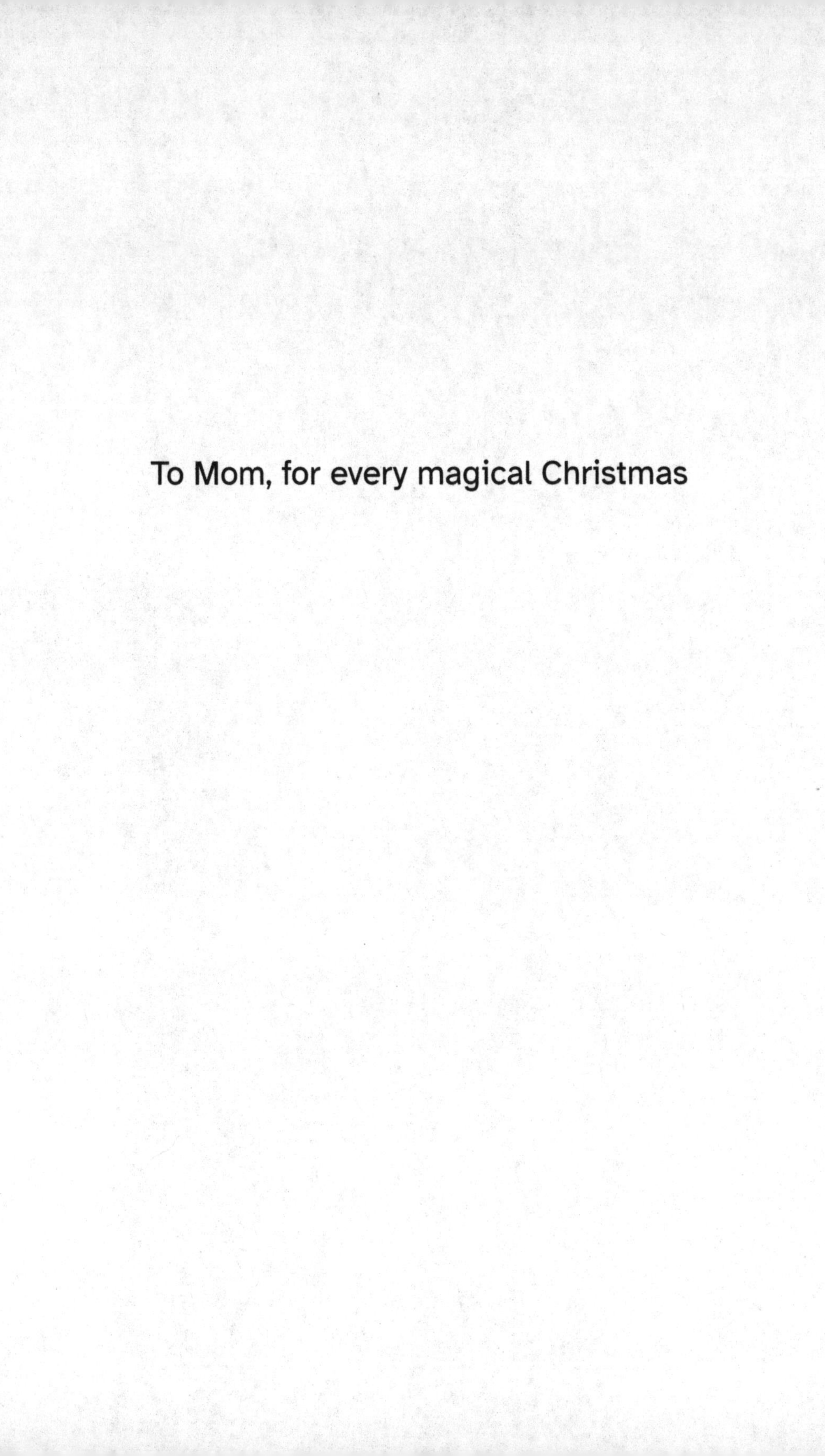

To Mom, for every magical Christmas

At least I'll never see last night's terrible hookup again, right?

My evening with the sexy bartender may have started off hot, but it ended in disaster. I should've known she was too good to be true. What a relief to put the whole disappointing encounter in my rearview as I head home for the holidays.

But guess who ends up fighting me for the last rental car on the lot when a blizzard shuts down all air travel three days before Christmas? Looks like my nightmare one-night-stand and I are in for the world's most awkward road trip if I want to make it to Chicago in time for eggnog.

But as Birdy and I cross state line after state line in this shoebox-sized car, I start to think my first instinct was right: this girl could be the one.

And I'm going to convince her of that, even if it takes a miracle.

Contents

Chapter 1

Sebastian

I'm desperately trying to hang onto my shitty mood, but the bartender's making it tough.

"Goddamn," the man next to me mutters, his gaze fixed on her ass.

I agree, but I don't say so. For one thing, that guy's being gross enough for both of us. And for another thing, I'm not going to be in town long enough to form an opinion about the bartender one way or another.

"Wonder when she gets off?" My disgusting neighbor rubs his palms over his khaki-clad thighs, and I don't need to be an expert in male-male communication to know what's going to cross his fleshy lips next. "'Cause we'll both be getting off about ten minutes after that."

Even though the bar's noisy and she's a few feet away slicing limes with breathtaking speed and precision, the bartender swivels just enough to catch my gaze. She must've heard his comment because she flashes me a look of such amused horror that I have to bite my lips to keep from chuckling. Why she's made me her silent conspirator, I don't know, but she's been doing it all night, sending me these sly little glances full of mirth and intelligence. We've only exchanged a few sentences, but it's almost like I have a direct pipeline to the thoughts tumbling through her brain: *Can you believe this guy?* her gorgeously funny face seems to say. *Lucky for him I'm in a good mood even though my feet are killing me.*

The last of my irritation drains away as I absorb the silent monologue she's sending me, and I tilt my head to give my silent response: *This isn't worth your time. I got this.* Then I take a sip of my beer and divert this guy as hard as my flight was diverted from Logan International a few hours earlier.

"What's the deal with the decor?" I gesture at the carved ostrich head mounted over the far end of the bar. Its wooden feathers are painted purple, green, and orange, and impressively long lashes frame its blue gemstone eyes. A hot pink feather boa's draped around its neck, and earrings dangle from its head where the ears would be.

The change of subject does the trick. My neighbor's glassy gaze swims past me to land on the drag queen ostrich, and his ruddy face splits into a smile. "Oh, that's Miss Gouda. She's the patron saint of the bar. Pretty cunning, huh?"

"Never seen anything like her," I agree as the bartender moves through the periphery of my vision. As gaudily fantastic as Miss Gouda is, she doesn't hold a candle to the woman slinging drinks. The bartender's got blue eyes that rival the ostrich's sapphires, and she's dressed like a Christmas gift in a tight red dress with a green bow headband nestled in her blonde curls. The bow should look juvenile on someone who I'd guess is in her late 20s, but instead she's festive and adorable. And, yes, fuckable. My neighbor isn't wrong about that.

When I landed my plane in Burlington, Vermont, and not Boston as scheduled, I grudgingly acknowledged that I'd be stuck there overnight. So I accepted my fate and hopped into a Lyft from the airport, asking the driver to take me someplace where I could knock back a drink while I sulked in peace.

Well, mission not accomplished, Lyft-driver Travis. This well-cared-for little bar was supposed to be a place for me to kill an hour or two before I find my hotel, collapse, and hopefully make my way to Chicago tomorrow. Instead, four hours have passed, and I'm still here.

The drinks are strong, and they're not too expensive. The barstool is comfortable. The music's the perfect mix of classic rock and Christmas tunes. It's just crowded enough that the space is warm and buzzy despite the New

England cold that leaks in every time the bell jingles to let in another patron. But none of those things are the reason that I still have an elbow propped against the bar.

It's *her*. This holiday angel slinging drinks a foot away makes it impossible for me to spend the night feeling sorry for myself. She focused only on me when I gave her my order, and she danced as she mixed it. Not in a showy way, not like she was aware that every eye in the place was on her. All night long, the smooth motion of her hips is uninhibited and solely for herself, as if she can't help but move to music only she can hear.

She's just so... alive. She's the only person working the bar, and somehow she's keeping us all in drinks and good cheer without a single ripple of stress in her entire body. She's a magnet and we're the metal shavings, trembling and surging toward her when she sweeps down the center of the horseshoe-shaped bar, where eyes fix on her from both sides of the mellow wood. Even me, who planned to spend tonight sulking because I'm currently stranded hundreds of miles away from my family days before Christmas thanks to a series of blizzards disrupting every flight east of the Mississippi.

As the night wears on and Bing and Elvis disagree about what color Christmas we can expect, I watch a handful of other patrons shoot their shot. They ask for her digits or slide her an inviting smile. Flex their biceps or curl a lock of hair around a finger. And the bartender just lights up with a sparkling grin before spinning away to mix another drink with an ease that speaks to hours behind the bar. The confidence I have at the controls of a Boeing 767, that's what she's got with bottles and bitters.

"Another?"

She doesn't lift her head from where she's pouring vodka into a shaker, but her eyes flick up to mine, bright and playful under velvety lashes.

The jolt of electricity I feel forces the corner of my mouth to curl upward.

"Sure." Why even pretend? I've been putty in her hands all night long, along with at least half of the patrons here. I slap a twenty on the bar.

"It looks like Miss Gouda could use a tiara. Buy her something nice."

"Only if I can buy myself a matching one." Her bright red lips tilt upward as she pockets the cash and gets back to mixing the martinis.

"And replace the Christmas bow? No deal." I wiggle my fingers at her. "Give it back."

She straightens the green headband with a wink and deposits the drinks in front of a group of women a few stools over. "Too late. Gouda and I are getting tiaras."

Before I can respond, she's poured me a fresh beer with the perfect head of foam and whirled away in a cloud of blonde hair to serve the college kids who just came in. She sets out a row of shot glasses and with a showy flick of her wrist is pouring tequila down the line without even looking as the boys rowdily cheer her on. When the last one overflows and spills onto the wood, she bursts into laughter as she pulls the bottle away, ending up with a splash of tequila running down her fingers.

"Want me to lick that off for you?" asks one of the older guys who's been drinking steadily all night. He stretches over the bar with a leer and catches her wrist. I straighten immediately, prepared to remove his grubby, overly eager hands from her body, but she stops me with one quick head shake. Every relaxed line of her body tells me she's got this. And she does.

"Your mother taught you better manners than that," she says, lightly smacking his hand away.

"Ah, c'mon, Birdy. Don't be like that." He flops back onto his chair and pushes a hank of hair out of his eyes. "We could have some fun after you close up, yeah?"

Her laughing eyes slide over to mine, and this time, it's like she can hear *my* thoughts: *That guy has no idea how to handle a woman like you. Neither do the frat boys snickering nearby.*

But I do. I know *exactly* how to handle a woman like her.

Playful, bold, talkative, joyful... sweet baby Jesus, sex with her would be magnificent. What a shame she lives in Vermont and I live in Michigan. She's exactly the kind of woman I've spent the last year trying to find.

She's also the kind of woman who knows how to handle a handsy drunk.

"I think it's time to cut you off, Jimbo." For the first time all night, there's steel at the edge of her smile as she whisks away his half-finished beer and sets a glass of water in front of him. "That goes for you too."

It takes a bit for me to realize she's looking my way.

"Me?" My brows lift in surprise as she plunks a club soda in front of me, dropping in a lemon slice and a straw. Then she disappears to the opposite end of the bar, and I push away that rogue fantasy of unwrapping her like an early Christmas gift. No idea why she cut me off, but she's not wrong that I'll probably sleep better without extra alcohol sloshing around my system.

Half an hour later, I'm glad to have a clear head because the frat boys have goaded each other into playing the same Taylor Swift song on repeat, and the bartender and I trade mock-horrified expressions.

"Twice was great," she murmurs, topping off my drink as the jangly intro kicks up again.

I lift it in a toast to the jukebox. "Seven times is too damn much."

But just as quickly as we lock eyes, she's moving down the bar to serve another thirsty patron, leaving me with my club soda and a nice view of her legs in that short red dress.

Before I know it, it's 2 a.m., and the bar's almost emptied out. I should've been back at my hotel ages ago. The last time I was at a bar this late, I was being charming as fuck to a group of women at a bachelorette party, and it paid off handsomely. Tonight, though, I'm content just to exist and contemplate Miss Gouda. There's wisdom in those fake sapphire eyes.

Red flashes at the edge of my vision, breaking into my comfortable cocoon of warmth and low lights and vintage Christmas tunes. The bartender leans her elbows on the bar in front of me and props her chin in her hands, shooting me one of those megawatt smiles.

"Want to give me fifteen minutes to close up and then we can get out of here?"

I blink. "Sorry, what?" I have to be misunderstanding her.

Her glossy red lips twist into a crooked smile. "I mean, you don't have to. But there's a reason I switched you to water a while back."

Surprise hits me first, followed closely by an excited buzz that has nothing to do with alcohol. "Oh yeah?"

"I want you on your game." She lifts one shoulder and lets it fall as my hungry eyes track the graceful movement. "Whaddya say?"

I'm so surprised by the unexpected offer that I don't respond immediately, and she twists her lips into a playful pout.

"Wow, are you really gonna make me beg?"

Fuck it. There's a chance I'm not going to make it home for Christmas, so this is the gift I'm giving myself.

"I'll help clear the tables."

Chapter 2

Sebastian

"Birdy? That's your name, right?"

We're bundled together in the back of a Lyft, and I don't even care that the driver's eyes are fixed on us in the rearview mirror, clearly enjoying the spectacle of a one-night stand about to get underway.

"It is." Her voice is amused, her eyes alight, and for a moment it looks like she's not even going to bother asking for mine like it's a game we're playing. But after a beat, she raises her brows. "And you are...?"

"Sebastian St. Claire."

"Wow. First *and* last."

I brush my thumb against the back of her neck and lean close to murmur, "Just giving you options to shout later."

I almost hate to drop such a blatant line, but it works. Her eyes flare, the sexy confidence that drew my eye in the bar rolling off her in waves. I'm grateful for it. Once I slid into the backseat of this car with her, I wondered if she'd rethink her surprise offer. I'd be fine if she did, obviously, but I'm so damn glad she didn't.

"Here you go," the driver says, and I pull my eyes away from Birdy to see we've come to a stop in front of my brightly lit Marriott.

"I take it you're not from around here?" Birdy says.

"Nope. That okay?"

"Perfect."

The driver snickers softly at our exchange. "Have a good night, you two," he calls as I slide out and shut the door behind me with a quick "Thanks." The car glides away, and I make an "after you" gesture, stepping through the sliding glass doors into the dim stillness of the lobby right behind her. We walk quickly past the young, sleepy-looking hotel clerk who barely acknowledges us as I summon the elevator. Neither of us speaks while it dings its way to the ground floor, and as I press the button for the fifth floor, I glance over at her, then snap my mouth shut.

She raises her brows in a question. "What?"

Well, if she really wants to know...

"Why me? Out of everybody at the bar?" I probably sound needy, but just like with the Lyft driver, I can't bring myself to care. I'm curious about what makes this beautiful girl tick.

Now she's the one hesitating before she speaks. Her gaze drops to the floor, and she almost seems to deflate. Then she lifts her chin, her cocky smile back in place.

"Your eyes are pretty," she says. "And you didn't seem likely to unalive me."

I bark a laugh as the doors open to our floor, and I steer her to the right. "No unaliving tonight. Plus, I used my Lyft app, and all these hotel lobbies have cameras."

I don't bother with the *I don't usually do things like this* as I usher her into my hotel room, and neither does she. True or not, it doesn't matter tonight. I'm using this sexy, charismatic girl to scrub away my frustration at being stuck in Vermont, and as I slip my hands under her coat to slide it off her shoulders, I briefly wonder what she's using *me* for.

"Do you want to hit the bathroom first?" I ask, pointing to the door to our left. "Or we could turn on the TV and—"

Without warning, she grabs my face and kisses me, and it dissolves the last bit of politeness that kept me from reaching for her the instant the door shut behind us. I grab her hips and haul her against me. I'm already hard, and I want her to know that she did this to me with this first touch. Because she kisses like she bartends: assertive, flirty, playful. Her tongue makes bold strokes as her fingers tunnel through my hair, and she uses her grip to tilt my head where she wants it, sliding her lips along mine. She's in control, and I love it. Then she shoves me back with a quick push to my chest, and before I can ask if everything's okay, she's unzipping her dress and sliding it to her waist, leaving her in a plain black bra.

"Shit," I breathe. It's not articulate, but it's the best I can do as she shimmies the red material over her hips to the floor, her breasts jutting out as she does, and I have to say it again. *Have* to. "Shit, Birdy."

Like her bra, her panties are more sensible than fantasy, but that doesn't mean they're not hot as fuck. And good for her for not working all night with a thong wedged up her ass. All those curves are gorgeous no matter what she's wrapped in.

When she reaches up to remove the cute-as-hell green Christmas bow nestled in her blonde hair, I touch her wrist. "Leave it on?"

She rolls her eyes. "I'm nobody's present." She yanks it off and tosses it aside, but my disappointment is short-lived when she toes off her shoes and whips the comforter back to reveal the crisp white sheets underneath. "Coming?" she asks.

"Hell yes." I kick off my shoes and strip out of my jeans, and then me, my boxer briefs, and my erection join her on the bed.

I stretch out next to her, intent on kissing her for as long as she'll let me because her lips are soft and her mouth is hot and each sweep of her tongue against mine fires my blood hotter. But after a disappointingly short time, she pulls away to press her teeth against the hollow under my ear.

"You kiss so good." She breathes into my skin. "I knew you would."

"You did?" God, she's turning me stupid. I can barely form a sentence when she's licking my jaw like that as she runs her foot up and down my calf.

"Not all boys with pretty eyes do," she breathily informs me. "But I had a hunch about you."

This seems like a good time to reach for the clasp on her bra. "I'm glad not to disappoint." I work the hooks and ease it down her arms, barely biting back yet another curse as her soft, full tits spill out. "Speaking of not disappointing…"

I flatten my hand against one of her breasts, enjoying the tight hardness of her nipple against my palm. She clearly enjoys it too, arching up and meeting my eyes with her own, big and pleading.

"Your mouth," she croons. "Please."

Like I'm saying no to that. But first I slip my finger between her lips, stroking along her tongue and using that wetness to just barely brush her nipples. Then I slide down to replace my finger with my mouth and let my hands explore her body as I suck on her nipple. Her back bows upward again as I slip my hand under the elastic of her panties, continuing downward until I reach her pussy. I brush the pad of one finger over her clit, lightly at first, gently, until her hips start to move. I slip my finger down further, where I find her wet. It's the go-ahead I'm looking for, and I slide my finger back to her clit and press harder, circling until I figure out the pressure that makes her gasp. But when I pull away from her breast to start kissing my way down her stomach, she stops me.

"No, I- I want…"

I look up at her, liquid heat coursing through my veins. I'm dying to feast on her pussy, but the wild joy I expect to see on her face isn't there. The teasing, tempting smile is gone, replaced with a creased brow and a frown.

"What can I do?" My voice is rough as I give her clit another pass with the tip of my finger.

She shakes her head restlessly, her brow knotting further and her hair catching against the starchy pillowcase. "I just… I want to be filled up." She looks at me with something like helplessness. "I'm so tired of being empty. Can you fill me up?"

"God yes," I breathe, and I wish I could say I wasn't clumsy as I roll off the bed to rummage through my travel kit for a condom, but hell, my dick's hard as fucking steel at the raw breathiness in her voice, and it makes my movements rushed. Once I'm suited up, I crawl back on the bed and settle between her legs.

Her chest is heaving as she sucks in deep breaths, and I nudge her knees further apart, gripping my dick and guiding it toward her entrance. "You're sure? I can make you come first. Make sure it's great for you."

Another shake of her head. She's all impatient hunger now, grabbing for me, pulling me close, urging me on.

"Please," she croons. "I need... I need..."

The words strangle in her throat, and I do as I'm told. Somehow, I'm what she needs tonight, so I'm going to give it to her. I push forward, sliding into all that wet and heat, a groan tearing from my throat as I do.

"Jesus, you feel good." I barely pause once I'm fully seated, pulling out so I can push in again. If she wants to be stuffed full of me, I'm happy to oblige, over and over and over.

She throws her head back as her hips rise to meet mine. Her eyes are screwed shut, but she grabs my shoulders, her nails digging into my skin as she pants. "Yes. Harder. Fuck, *harder*!"

So I do it harder. I set a steady pace and let myself enjoy the friction of moving in her body, cupping her breast, licking a bead of sweat off her jaw as she twists under me.

This isn't the playful encounter I was expecting based on our interactions at the bar, but it's still hot as fuck. I don't think anybody's ever been this frantic for me before, and it's incredible.

"Can you come for me?" I rasp into her ear. I can already feel my orgasm approaching, the tension gathering at the base of my spine, tightening my balls. It's happening too fast, but I'll be goddamned if I get there first.

"I need... I need... need..." She's chanting the word, her fingers clawing at the sheets, so I reach between us and press my finger to her clit. But I only circle it twice before she grabs my wrist and pushes my fingers even harder against her.

"*Yes,*" she cries, and thank God for the pulses and flutters I feel against my cock because it means I can let go too. And I do, surging forward one last time and groaning as I empty myself into the condom.

Once the tremors have finished running through my body, I fall back against the bed with a breathless laugh. She rolls so she's facing the wall, and I run my hand down the overheated skin of her back.

"God*damn*," I gasp out. "That was hot."

A tremor runs down her spine, and because I'm post-orgasm and all my systems are offline, it takes me a little too long to realize that she's crying.

I scramble upright.

"Birdy?" Alarm makes my voice sharp as she curls into herself, her shoulders hunching inward as a hoarse cry bursts from her throat.

"Hey, are you okay?" I risk a touch to her shoulder because Christ, I can't let her cry alone, this woman I just had sex with and apparently horrified to tears. I run my hand down her back in what I hope is a soothing motion as she sobs brokenly.

"I've got you," I murmur as she shudders under my fingertips. I have no idea what I'm trying to comfort her for, but eventually her tears slow and she sucks in a huge breath, jerking away to angrily swipe at the wet tracks on her cheeks.

"I'm sorry," she gasps, and it's a completely different gasp than the ones she made with me not three minutes ago.

She slides off the bed and darts to the pile of clothes on the floor.

I stand too, keeping enough of a distance not to crowd her. "Did I do something?" I ask. "*Can I do something?*"

"No." She's already pulling her red dress on, and her voice is muffled as she slides it over her head. "And no."

Her head pops free, and she bats her tousled hair away from her face, then reaches for her shoes while I stand there like an idiot. A naked idiot.

"I don't understand what's happening here," I say, feeling like my brain's operating at half speed.

Her jerky movements don't stop as she slides into her coat.

"I thought this was what I needed tonight," she says, her voice still thick with tears, "but clearly I was wrong."

Her eyes stray toward the rumpled bed, then dip back to me. Still naked. A flush touches her cheeks, and she lifts her chin. Her eyes are watery, and her nose is red, but her spine is straight. "I'm sorry if this was, like, traumatic for you."

Then she turns and heads toward the door. My moment of frozen shock dissolves, and I wrap the sheet around my waist and follow her.

"Wait," I call, but she's already in the hallway, and I lower my voice out of respect for the rest of the hall. It's got to be 3 a.m. by now. "Just stay," I say in a raised whisper from the doorway.

She looks over her shoulder at me, her eyes wet and sad. "Why?"

My mouth opens, but no answers come. It's not like I can promise to make things better since I have no idea what set her off in the first place. And clearly my presence isn't helping anyway.

She uses my silence to move further down the hallway, where she mashes her finger against the elevator button. I'm tempted to follow her, but my room key's somewhere in the mess of my clothes, and I'm wrapped in a sheet with the condom still on my fucking dick. I'm in no condition to chase her down.

The elevator dings as it slides open, and she inhales hard before glancing my way again.

"Thanks." She shoots me a little smile, and I see a ghost of the mischievous girl from the bar in it. "For what it's worth, I still think you're a great kisser."

With that, she steps onto the elevator and disappears, leaving me with no last name, no phone number, no way to reach her other than to show back up at the bar, which is closed since we're only a couple of hours away from sunup by now. I assume I could catch her outside the hotel waiting for her rideshare, but if she wanted to hear from me again, she wouldn't have burst into tears and literally fled, would she?

"Shit."

I mutter the word as I turn back to the room and let the door fall shut behind me. My heart's still pounding from the sex followed by the adrenaline of my partner bursting into sobs. The whole situation's so surreal that for a second, I almost wonder if I made it all up, like I wasn't actually diverted from Boston and I didn't actually end up at a magical little bar where I took home maybe the prettiest girl I'd ever seen. It all feels like a dream.

But no. There on the nondescript hotel room carpet is Birdy's green bow headband.

I stoop to pick it up, twirling it between my fingers as I head to the bathroom to clean myself up, not sure I'll get any sleep tonight at all.

Chapter 3

Birdy

I thought growing up in a bar prepared me for pandemonium, but it's nothing compared to a regional airport facing down a string of blizzards four days before Christmas.

"Next!"

The voice cuts through my noise-blocking earbuds, and I pluck them out and step forward, relieved to separate myself from the packed, jostling crowd that's been knocking me from side to side all morning. We're all overheating in our coats, and we left polite behind the instant we stepped through the airport doors to discover that basically all of our flights have been canceled.

I step forward, limp with relief at finally making it to the front of the rental car line, and remove the sunglasses hiding my red, puffy eyes.

"Hi," I tell the statuesque woman whose nametag says ROCHELLE. "I'm hoping to rent a car."

Rochelle snorts. It's quiet, but it carries an ocean of derision. "Unless you have a reservation, you're out of luck. Every airport from here to Denver is shut down or about to, which means—sorry, hold on." She snatches the phone in front of her from its cradle, snapping a terse, "Yes?"

I set down my bulky canvas bag next to my wheeled suitcase and shift my overstuffed weekender from my aching left shoulder to my less-sore right one. My gaze fixes on the garland of holly berries drooping from the counter, an attempt at holiday cheer that's unwelcome in my current state.

As I wait for Rochelle, one cell phone conversation in particular rises above the sea of humanity amassing behind me.

"You're kidding," a frustrated voice snaps. "There's not a single flight you can get me on? Not to anywhere in the Midwest? Like at all?" After a pause in which I'm grateful that he's at least not having this conversation on speakerphone, the man groans. The sound is rich, throaty, and... distantly familiar?

I pray for the guy to end his loud conversation as I swipe at my sweaty forehead under my battered Red Sox cap. It's zero degrees outside and nine hundred degrees inside. I may die in here.

The guy behind me gives another groan that pings something in the depths of my brain, then gives a clipped, "Thanks for trying, Jan."

Rochelle's also off the phone by now, and I open my mouth to offer her my thrifted Chanel bag, my stack of Kohl's cash, and naming rights to my firstborn. Whatever she wants if she'll just get me out of this boiling airport and in a car and on my way. But before I can start bartering, Rochelle's eyes fix on something over my shoulder, and her frown dissolves into a bright smile. "Hello, captain. How can I help you?"

Captain?

The loud phone call man steps up next to me at the counter. I pointedly angle my body away from him, hoping the disapproving lines of my back send the silent message of *wait your turn, asshole.*

It doesn't work.

"Any chance you've got a rental car to spare?" he asks Rochelle. "You're my only hope."

I slide my eyes to the side far enough to see the edge of a dark suit sleeve with gold stripes on the arm, then snap them back when Rochelle shakes her head.

"As I was just telling this customer"—she half-heartedly gestures toward me, but I'm too exhausted from the past twenty-four hours to straighten up and look intimidating—"everybody's scrambling, and we're simply out of stock."

Well, well. Guess even the pilots are going to be stuck in Vermont for longer than they wanted.

"Are you sure there isn't anything? A car that's been checked in but not processed yet?" The man's voice is warm and enticing and again, it pings something in my brain. "See, my sister's boyfriend's proposing to her on Christmas morning at my parents' house in Chicago, and I promised him I'd be there for moral support."

That suit-clad elbow comes to rest on the counter inches from mine, and I'm so annoyed I'm tempted to shove it off. Also, why does his exasperated voice sound familiar?

"That's the sweetest thing!" Rochelle's face brightens like the Christmas tree that the captain's family will presumably be gathered around in holiday bliss once he's back in their warm embrace. She glances around at the chaos of the airport. People are mobbing the competing car rental counters on either side of us, and the crowd behind me and the captain is getting ever bigger. She bites her lip and pokes at the keyboard in front of her, then drops her voice. "It looks like we do have one vehicle that was returned but hasn't been cleaned and processed yet. I could—"

"I'll take it," the man announces. And that's when I get mad.

"Wait a minute!" I blurt. "I was here first."

I sound childish and whiny, but dammit, I *was* here before this man with his golden wings came strolling in. I finally turn to face him, prepared to tell him to step the eff back, but when I do, the pretty eyes looking back at me shut me right up.

"You," I manage to croak out.

"Shit. Hi." Those dark eyes widen in surprise, and now I know why his groans sound so familiar. He pressed them into my skin only a few hours ago when we were both naked.

Embarrassment crawls up my throat, and I blurt, "How did you—" at the same time he says, "What are you—"

"Does one of you want the car?" Rochelle asks, her eyes narrowing at the crowd starting to grumble loudly behind us.

"Yes," we shout at the same time.

"I'll take it." He jerks a thumb at me. "She lives around here."

"What makes you think that?" I demand, my discomfort momentarily forgotten.

He gestures out the big airport window. "I dunno, the fact that you work at a bar eight minutes from here?"

Grief swamps me, and I whisper, "You don't know anything about me," sucking in a shaky breath as he eyes me uneasily, no doubt wondering if I'm going to burst into tears again. I'm almost tempted to do it if it means I might get a rental car out of it, but I'm better than that. Probably.

Rochelle's eyes now move from him to me, and her lips tighten. "You've got thirty seconds to figure out who's signing for it."

We glare at each other until she sighs. "One car. It's what I've got. I'm sure any of the people behind you would be glad to take it off your hands."

Mutters of agreement rumble down the line, I don't have to look around to know the angry mob ready to pull out their torches and pitchforks.

With one last, furious look at the would-be car thief, I say firmly, "I was here first." I angrily zip open my purse and rummage through it for my wallet.

Kleenex. Lip gloss. Mints. Extra pair of socks. Sunglasses, which are going to be super handy in a blizzard.

No wallet.

"Oh hell," I breathe, pawing through the bag in desperation. "Dammit!"

I upend the whole bag onto the floor of the airport, not even flinching when an avalanche of loose pennies plink on the floor next to a stray tampon. "Come on!" I wail, close to crying for real this time.

"Ma'am," Rochelle says disapprovingly, "if you don't have the proper documentation, I'm afraid I can't rent you a car."

"No, it's..." I gesture helplessly at the contents of my purse, then the overstuffed weekender bag and lumpy canvas tote on the ground next to my feet. Shit, did I stash my wallet in one of them after leaving the title company this morning? Or maybe in my suitcase? "It's in here somewhere, I swear."

The crowd behind me undulates like a large, dangerous animal, and I hear someone growl, "Come the fuck *on*, lady," and someone else shouts, "I've got *my* ID right here."

Blinking back tears, I start to paw through my weekend when goddamn *Captain* Sebastian St. Claire kneels to scoop my belongings off the airport floor.

Sebastian St. Claire. What a ridiculously perfect name for the man with the gorgeous eyes and the shiny hair and the talented fingers.

"Where are you trying to get to?" he asks quietly, and I pointedly do not think about the fact that he's shoving a tampon back into my purse.

"Milwaukee," I mutter.

Those eyes narrow in thought, and then he says, "Okay. Go with me on this."

He stands and fishes his wallet out of his pocket. By the time I've restored all my belongings into some kind of order, he's filled out all the paperwork and is accepting keys and a carbon copy of his rental agreement.

"Come on." He shoulders my two biggest bags, then takes my arm with the hand that isn't gripping his wheelie suitcase. "We might get rolled for these keys if we don't get out of here."

"We... what?" I'm almost jogging to keep up with his long legs, but he doesn't slow as he hauls me toward the exit. "What's happening?"

"We're getting our rental car."

"Check it out. That's Santa suit red." Sebastian pats the hood of the tiniest Chevrolet I've ever seen.

All I can manage is a grunt.

My mortification grew and grew during our walk to the rental car lot, and I'm close to combusting from the awkwardness of standing next to this man. His jawline's even more well-defined in the daylight, and his lips are even lusher and more kissable. I was never supposed to see him again. I was never even supposed to *think* about last night again. But here he is, and Mr. Saw-Me-At-My-Lowest-Point is even better looking in the daylight.

He glances up at the oppressive gray sky stretching over the rental car lot.

"We need to get moving. We're maybe an hour ahead of the snow, and I want to keep it that way."

"You seriously expect me to ride with you all the way to Chicago?" I sound stubborn, hostile even, but his plan makes no damn sense.

"Sure." The icy wind ruffles his thick brown hair as he dumps his bag and then mine into the trunk. "You can grab a train to Milwaukee from Union Station."

I have no idea why he's going out of his way to help me. He should be running in the opposite direction of the crazy chick he took home from the bar, but instead he's proposing we drive mile after uncomfortable mile together.

"What's wrong with you?" Embarrassment has me blurting out the question, but I cannot fathom why he'd volunteer to spend one more second in my company after the absolute meltdown I had while we were naked.

His brows snap together in confusion.

Wait, no. That's anger.

"I am being *nice*," he bites out, unzipping his suitcase to retrieve a puffer jacket that he tosses into the back seat. Unlike last night, I don't see any warmth in his eyes. Those soft, pretty eyes that followed me all night long at the bar, amused and appreciative without ever bordering on creepersville.

The guy with the nice eyes had seemed like a pretty good dude, and as the night wore on, I began to imagine that he and I were in a club of two thanks to our shared smiles and conspiratorial glances. I'm the girl who's sworn off anything deeper than easy breezy hookups, but last night I wanted to hold onto that feeling of connection a little bit longer. To have someone on my team for a few more hours before I officially moved into the world alone.

And look how great that went. Not only did he see me lose control, but he was so kind about it. I've spent too much time around drunk, handsy men to not be surprised by that. And even before that, he seemed genuinely cool and fun. *I* was the mess he tried to clean up last night, and now he's volunteering to escort that mess halfway across the country.

He must be regretting it now though; his jaw is tense and hard as he says, "Come with me or don't." He jabs a finger at the tarmac, where row after row of planes sits idle. "But I don't see that you have a ton of other choices."

"Because you stole my car," I snap.

"She wasn't going to give you this car," he snaps back. "She only offered it to me when I pushed, and she only did *that* because of *this*." He jabs a finger at the golden wings on his lapel. "You're welcome."

I roll my eyes. "Thank you, *captain*. How generous of you."

His jaw tightens even more, and he grits out, "I've got places to be, so I'm leaving. If you're not coming along, get your bags out of the trunk."

With that, he turns on his heel and stalks to the driver's side, sliding behind the wheel and firing up the engine.

The petulant part of me wants to let him drive away so I can put this all behind me, tuck it all into a deep, dark box and submerge it in the Mariana Trench. But I don't see any other way to get back to Wisconsin anytime soon. A nor'easter tearing up the East Coast is paralyzing every airport in its path, and a massive storm system from the Rockies to the Great Plains is doing similar damage to Midwestern travel. I don't even know if the highways will be passable at this point. Getting into Sebastian's car is the only option I can see.

Swallowing back a scream, I slam the trunk shut and drag myself to the passenger side. I'm sure neither of us can conceive of anything more awkward than being trapped in that tiny car with a hookup gone wrong for hundreds of miles.

Sure enough, Sebastian's eyes are straight ahead, his hands gripping the wheel at 10 and 2. "Seatbelt," is all he says.

I click it and slide my earbuds into my ears. Maybe if I try really, really hard, I can imagine I'm anywhere but here.

Chapter 4

Sebastian

What's wrong with *me*? More like what's wrong with *her*?

It's not like I stole her fucking rental. Rochelle wasn't going to offer her this car. As it often does, my uniform opened a door that would've stayed closed if I'd been in jeans and a T-shirt. But the tight-lipped woman ignoring me from the passenger seat doesn't seem to be in the mood for a debate about it.

Christ, what did I do last night that had her running out the door? I open my mouth to ask her, then snap it shut. What explanation could she give that's going to improve the mood in this car? I was hoping we could both pretend like it never happened. We could be strangers stuck together in a shitty holiday travel situation. But she shot that down in about five seconds flat.

What's wrong with you?

I wish I knew. The first girl in ages I actually liked, and it ended in tears and disaster. And now I get to inhale her shampoo and think about how cute she is in her jeans and an oversized University of Wisconsin sweatshirt for hundreds of miles.

I set the car in motion while she's staring pointedly out her window, and as we leave Burlington in our rearview, silence becomes the third passenger.

I've always been guilty of making snap judgments about people and clinging to them. Some might even say I cling to my first impressions beyond what's reasonable. My sister, for example, would remind me that I almost blew it for her when I met her boyfriend last Christmas. But wow did the woman now sullenly scrolling through her phone end up having none of the qualities I imagined she did. She went from dream girl to sobbing mess to hostile nightmare, and we've got fifteen hours in this car together—and that's if we're lucky with the weather.

The thought spikes my nerves, and I stomp on the gas. We made it out of town before the snow hit, but now, about an hour into our journey, flakes start to drift from the sky. I press my foot down harder, already calculating how much daylight we have left. It's just past noon, so if—

"In forty-six miles, you'll see an exit for Stilson Grove. Take it."

"Come again?"

I glance over at her, and her eyes are straight ahead, fixed on the road. She's traded her battered ball cap for a thick knit hat with a pompon the size of my fist. "I found a rental place with an available car."

"You're kidding."

At my disbelieving scoff, she glances over, and I see in the flat line of her mouth that she's not asking, she's telling.

"The internet's a miraculous thing," she deadpans. "It's only a short detour, and then I won't be your problem anymore."

I want to argue with her. Tell her the snow's going to catch up with us if we stop at this point. Tell her it's ridiculous for her to rent her own car when she's already in one that's headed in the right direction. Tell her that I need to know what I did last night that was so fucking terrible.

"You're that desperate to run away from me again?" It slips out, and I pray she doesn't hear the hurt curling around my words.

Thankfully, she merely exhales and says, "Just take the exit. Please."

Why am I fighting this? I can be free of this awkward situation within the hour. I tighten my hands on the wheel and nod curtly. "Fine."

I thought the silence was bad before? It was nothing compared to now. We drive like that for the next forty minutes, the mileposts flashing by as we barrel down the highway. I do as she asks, taking the Stilson Grove exit as the snow starts falling faster. We spend an eternity on a two-lane road that takes us into a barely-there town: a few blocks of houses, some fast-food places, a white stone courthouse on the town square, and...

"This is it?" Skepticism curls around my voice as I pull up in front of a run-down little storefront that Birdy's phone directed us to. Quality Car Rentals is painted on the big glass window, and the island of cracked asphalt around it is empty except for a rusty PT Cruiser and an oversized inflatable Santa with demonic yellow eyes.

"Apparently it is," she says, and the instant I put it into park, she tugs her hat down over her ears and grabs the wallet she managed to unearth from the depths of one of her huge bags on our walk to the car. When she flings open the door and starts walking toward the entrance, I barely hesitate before pocketing the keys and following her inside.

"Hi," she says once she's in the shop, brushing snow from her sleeves and unzipping her coat. "I'm Elizabeth Denton. I've got an online reservation."

"Reservation?" The piggy little eyes of the guy behind the counter travel down her body in such a gross, obvious way that I'm no longer second-guessing my decision to come inside with her.

She maintains her smile, and I'm no expert, but I don't think it's the real deal. Too stiff around the edges. Plus she zips her coat back up like she's picking up the same bad vibes I am. How could she not? I've never seen such a sketchy place in all my days renting cars. Behind the peeling linoleum of the counter, the back wall's only decoration is a calendar that's three years out of date, and bafflingly, along the far side of the room sits a row of dented washers and dryers with price tags.

"Just to clarify, you're a car rental company?" I'm still in my pilot's jacket, but unlike Rochelle, this guy doesn't look like he gives a shit about a uniform.

Sure enough, he curls his lip into a sneer and taps a sign bearing the name of a national car rental chain. It's curled and dirty around the edges, but it does promise that this place is authorized. "We're the only branch in the area."

Birdy clears her throat and glances through the window to the mostly empty parking lot. "Great. Well, I used your website to reserve a sedan."

The man lifts his hat to scratch at his peeling scalp. "Right. About that." His smile's as greasy as his forehead is dry. "Our online reservation system's... on the fritz."

I can smell the bullshit from a mile away. "So when will it be ready? Because I don't see any sedans on the lot." My tone is challenging, and the guy's thin lips flatten before he swings his attention back to Birdy.

"My employee took it to get detailed. Should be back before too long." His eyes rake down her body again. "It's just you wanting it? Not him?"

He jerks his head in my direction, and Birdy hesitates a beat before replying, "It's just me."

The guy's face splits into a grin that reveals mossy teeth. Christ, *I'm* uncomfortable. I can't imagine how she's keeping her cool. Yet she's standing there and taking it for some fucking reason.

"Tell you what," the guy says with a wink, "you just stay here with me, and Skip'll be back soon. Your friend doesn't need to wait with you."

Birdy and I both glance around the shop, and our eyes briefly catch. As annoyed as I am about this whole situation, I radiate *Are you sure about this?* as hard as I can in her direction. I watched her handle way less disgusting guys at the bar last night, so I'm waiting for her to metaphorically kick this jackass in the balls.

But the only movement is the flutter of her lashes as she shuts her eyes, closing us all out for a moment. Then she snaps them open and says, "Let me go grab my bags."

Disbelief swamps me. She's not going to tell this guy to fuck off. *This* situation is more preferable to her than traveling with me.

The guy licks his lips as he watches her push through the door and cross to our rental car, unholy interest burning in his gaze. I shift to stand between him and his view of Birdy's ass where she's bending over the trunk.

"So do you have a waiting area?" I demand.

The guy smirks and scratches his belly. "My office has a nice couch. She's welcome to it. Kick off her shoes, stretch out." He cranes his neck to look around me. "I can help her get *real* comfy."

The hell with that. She can ride the whole way to Chicago with me in miserable silence as far as I'm concerned, but I'm not leaving her here.

"No thanks." I stalk forward and grab Birdy's arm as she pushes back through the door. "We're leaving."

Her mouth opens in shock as I tug her back out the door over the guy's objections. "What are you doing?" she hisses as I usher her outside and yank the passenger door open.

"Saving you from being dismembered and fed to the possessed Santa, at best." I jab a thumb at the inflatable decoration, but Birdy's eyes travel past its round red belly to the window where the rental guy's glaring at us.

"What did he say while I was outside?" she asks almost hesitantly.

"Nothing you want me to repeat."

A shiver races through her, although that could as easily be from the cold as from the anger in the man's narrowed gaze. "Fine. Let's go." She slides into the passenger seat and slams the door shut.

"Glad to know I'm better than murder," I grumble to no one in particular as I walk around to the driver's side.

Silence falls over the car again as I put it into gear and roar out of the parking lot. As we rocket out of this hellhole, a bolt of longing hits me out of the blue. What if our night together had ended with laughter and cuddling and maybe another round of sex? What if she'd stuck around and we'd had a chance to talk about whatever sent her sprinting away? Maybe then we'd have been happy to split this rental car the next day. Maybe we'd be joking and flirting our way through an amazing road trip that would end with us exchanging numbers before reluctantly going our separate ways. Because for a few hours last night, the bold, laughing girl from the bar was exactly who I imagined one day bringing home to my family.

What is wrong with you?

Nothing, really, other than inventing fantasies in my head and then crashing to earth when the reality turns out to be way more disappointing.

Chapter 5

Birdy

I'm pissed.

I'm grateful.

I'm pissed about how grateful I am.

The rental car perv set off every one of my internal alarms, but I was prepared to ignore them if it meant getting away from the man currently trying to strangle the steering wheel. Not that I'm scared of Sebastian; I'm just realizing how much worse I made our already tense situation in the past hour. Being sacrificed to the big scary Santa at the rental place might've been preferable.

His terse voice breaks the silence. "If you find another rental company you want to try, let me know so I can budget time for a stop."

Then he stretches out his hand and flips on the radio to a station playing Christmas songs. It cuts off any response I might have made, although I'm tempted to tell him that I won't waste any more of his precious time trying to find an alternate ride. Handsome Sebastian St. Claire's made it clear that he's desperate to get home to his family. Are they the perfect little slice of American life? I picture a silver-haired mom and dad. A sister who shares his shiny dark hair. Oh God, what if he's married?

"You don't have a wife, right? Or a husband?"

I blurt my question, and his brows lift. "You're asking me this now?"

He has a point, and I shift uncomfortably. "Well? Do you?"

"No," he bites out. Conversation closed. It's abrupt enough that I almost ask what the story is there, but I remind myself that he's a stranger to me. A stranger who had his fingers in my mouth last night, sure, but a stranger.

"Same question, Elizabeth."

He hits my given name hard, and I barely hide my flinch.

"It's Birdy. And no."

His eyes cut over to me before he turns his attention back to the road. "Well that's one thing we didn't fuck up, anyway."

"Yay us." But some perverse part of me needs the last word. "Are we planning to drive through the night then?"

"Maybe," he snaps, not acknowledging that the drive to Chicago would be fourteen more hours on a good day. And with the storm picking up, today is not a good day.

The thought of that much more time in this car has me shivering. Plus it's freezing in here. The sun hasn't peeked through the clouds even once today, and with the temperature barely in single digits, I haven't truly felt warm since we left the airport. I lean forward and nudge the heat up a couple of degrees. The only good thing about today so far is that this car has a working heater.

Once I've adjusted it so I have a fighting chance of de-icicling my fingers, I swallow hard and do the thing I know I need to do next.

"Thanks for getting me out of that rental place." And now comes the tougher part. "Also, I'm sorry."

He immediately figures out what I'm referring to, and his knuckles whiten on the steering wheel. "You don't have to –"

"No, I do." I take a deep breath and speak to his handsome, frowning profile. "I'm sorry I wasted time on Stilson Grove, and I'm"—okay, here goes—"I'm also sorry about last night. None of that was because of you."

The only movement following my rush of words is a twitch of his eyebrows. "I think at least part of last night was because of me."

I huff out a startled laugh as my cheeks heat at the memory of the good parts he was responsible for.

"Yes, thank you, you were involved in the good parts," I say, resisting the urge to drop my eyes to my lap in embarrassment. "The rest of it..." I shift in my seat, not sure how much I wanted to share. "I was in town to handle some business with the bar, and it all caught up with me last night. The really great orgasm yanked the cork out of my emotions bottle, and I let it spill all over you, which wasn't fair. I'm really sorry about that."

"The cork on your...?"

"Emotions bottle, yeah." I shrug. "Don't you keep all your feelings bottled up so you don't end up overwhelmed and flat on your back?"

He gives a soft sigh. "Actually, I usually don't hold back. I'm not sure that's any better though."

It's as vulnerable as he's been since I first laid eyes on him, and it almost makes me wish things were different. That I was somebody interested in a boyfriend-type guy instead of someone getting rid of anything in her life that could possibly tie her down.

"Look at us and our healthy coping mechanisms," I murmur.

"Yeah, look at us." After a long moment, he slides me a cocky grin. "So it was a really great orgasm, huh?"

Of course that's what he took from our exchange. "Shut it," I say with an eye roll, although my core clenches at the memory of it. This conversation should make things even more awkward in this small, enclosed space, but things actually feel a little less tense than when we set out on this godforsaken journey.

Maybe it's just me feeling that way, though, because Sebastian suddenly mutters a curse.

"Grab the wheel for a sec."

I blink over in surprise, so he clarifies, "If you insist on keeping it 80 degrees in here, you're going to have to keep us on the road while I strip."

"While you... what?"

My hand moves faster than my brain, and I curl my fingers around the wheel as Sebastian tugs at the tie around his neck, loosening it until it slides out from under his collar. He leans toward me to shrug out of his coat, and I get a lungful of clean hair and pine trees. Then he tosses the jacket into the backseat as I fight the wind gusts to keep the car between the lines. That task gets harder when he starts on the buttons of his dress shirt, revealing the tight T-shirt underneath. Once all the buttons are undone, he leans over again to slide it off, and this time his shoulder brushes my arm. I jolt from the contact, and now my shivers definitely aren't from the cold.

"Thanks." He tosses the shirt over his shoulder and reclaims the wheel, his forearms flexing as his fingers dig into the leather.

I swallow hard and whip my gaze back to the road, flushing as I recall those strong wrists planted on either side of my head while he slid into me last night. If spontaneous human combustion really does exist, let it claim me now. I cannot be having those thoughts about the guy next to me, not when we have several more states to drive through before we can go our separate ways.

The reminder helps me get my body under control, and I wrap the silence back around myself and pray that the rest of the trip goes fast. That the snow lets up. That I don't toss myself out of the car to avoid these damn Christmas carols screeching from the radio.

At least I can control one of those things.

"No more sleigh bells," I announce, leaning forward to fiddle with the radio until it lands on a Top 40 station.

"Grinch," Sebastian replies, but his voice is relaxed, not mean.

"Yeah." I sit back and adjust my seatbelt so it falls more comfortably between my breasts. "Not feeling very Christmassy this year."

He sucks in a breath like he's about to ask for more details, but instead says, "If you find another place with a rental car, let me know."

"Oh. Okay." I don't know why, but my stomach drops in disappointment, which is ridiculous. I just dragged us on a wild goose chase trying to get out of his hair. He's being respectful of my wishes. I should be glad.

Then he clears his throat and adds, "But I really am fine driving you to Chicago."

"Um." The emotional whiplash of this conversation has knocked all of my conversational skills offline. All I can manage is, "Cool, thanks."

So he's good with this dynamic, then. The stilted conversation and the disagreement about the car's heater and the occasional flashes of what it felt like when his teeth grazed my skin.

Well if he can handle it, so can I. I desperately wish I could have a re-do on last night that didn't end quite so traumatically, but if he can be a normal person for a few hundred more miles, I can too, right?

There's no sound for a few minutes other than the wipers trying to keep up with the snow collecting on the windshield. Then Sebastian says, "The good news is, I love awkward silences."

I bleat out a laugh and clap my hands over my mouth to stifle the undignified sound. For a second I consider telling him everything: Lizzie leaving me the bar, the difficult decision to sell it, how I'm trying to move forward without her. But we're not here to share those kinds of secrets. So rather than let the intimacy of the moment deepen, I shut my mouth and let the silence take over again.

Chapter 6

Sebastian

"I know you've got a schedule, but can we stop to grab some food?"

Birdy's tentative voice cuts through the snow trance I'm in.

I blink at the dashboard clock. "Oh. Shit." It's almost 6, which means we've been driving for close to seven hours and we're not even to Rochester yet thanks to the heavy snowfall and gusting wind that's got us moving at a snail's pace. At this rate, the trip is going to take twice as long as GPS is telling us.

"Yeah, sure." Now that she brought it up, my stomach roars to life. "Sounds good."

We're in a worst-case-scenario travel situation with the storm making it tough to see the lane lines, and the muscles in my neck and back are screaming. Getting out of the car to walk for a bit will be good.

I take the next exit with signs promising a truck stop. When I pull up to the pump, Birdy chirps, "Bathroom!" and darts through the snow to the brightly lit store.

I grab my winter coat from the backseat and top off the tank, shivering as the wind gusts cut right through it. It was stupid of me not to pack a hat and gloves, but I'd assumed I'd be in and out of airports only on this trip. Once the pump spits out a receipt, I pull the car up to a spot outside the entrance and dash inside to find Birdy with her arms full of fruit and plastic-wrapped deli sandwiches.

"Roast beef, turkey, ham, and egg salad." She's cradling her haul like she would an infant. "I figured we could have a car picnic. Plus the oranges will keep us from getting scurvy."

"Okay, but is there chocolate?"

She gives me a *duh* face and juggles the food pile around until it reveals a stack of Reese's Peanut Butter Cups.

"Perfect." But I'm not talking about the chocolate. I'm talking about the pretty pink flush on her cheeks. Shit, I need to stop that. She's made it clear she's only spending time with me because I'm slightly less terrible than the rental car guy, so I'd like to *not* sink to his creepy level.

As we walk to the counter, a display of personalized tchotchkes catches my eyes, and I stop to poke through the brightly colored pencils and tiny New York license plates.

Birdy sends me a curious look, and I spin the rack as I scan the names. "If you see a Kayleigh spelled *kayleigh,* you'll make it so Uncle Seb wins Christmas."

"Uncle Seb?" she asks.

"Yep." I sort through the rows, finding Kayla and Kylie but no Kayleigh. "Damn. Poor kid can't ever find personalized stuff."

"I know that feeling," Birdy says drily, moving the sandwiches to the crook of one arm so she can poke through the rack next to the one I'm exploring.

"Oooh, look at this!" She triumphantly brandishes a little red airplane, sounding an awful lot like the vivacious bartender from last night. "You need it. You can hang it from your rearview mirror at work."

I take the plastic toy from her hand and turn it to see *Sebastian* printed on its body.

"Birdy," I ask in a voice I'd use with a precocious first grader, "do you think Boeings have rearview mirrors?" I'm rewarded with a full-throated laugh. I haven't heard it since last night, and despite everything that happened after, I'm transfixed.

"Well how else do you park them?" she asks, her voice all saucy innocence as she pokes at the toy dangling by its string from my fingers, making it spin. "This way you'll always know which cockpit is yours."

Now I'm laughing too, and I set it spinning in the opposite direction. "My copilot would be so jealous."

"If I was celebrating Christmas this year, I'd buy it for you."

Her smile dims, and before I make it weird by asking what's making her so sad, she says, "You ready?"

I nod and put the *Sebastian* plane back. "Ready." Overreach averted.

Once we're back on the road, we start in on the gas station sandwiches. I wish I knew what she was thinking as we do.

"So tell me about your niece."

Apparently she's thinking about my family.

"Three nieces, one nephew," I say, setting my half-eaten turkey sandwich down so I can have both hands on the wheel as we round a curve in the interstate. It's gotten even more treacherous while we were stocking up. We seem to be traveling the same path as the storm, and our progress is suffering because of it. "Ginny, Kayleigh, Madison, and Tristan. They're hell-beasts, and I love them."

"And your siblings?"

"They all belong to my oldest sister Celeste and her husband Aaron. Then my sister Darby's a year ahead of me."

"Is she the one getting engaged on Christmas morning?" I risk a glance at her, surprised she knows about that, and she shrugs. "You used it as a bargaining chip with Rochelle at the rental counter."

"Right." I wish I could feel worse about that, but it got me what I wanted. Maybe even more than that now that Birdy and I are having a semi-normal conversation. "That's Darby. I gave her boyfriend a hard time when I met him last Christmas, but we're tight now. I want to be there for it."

I really, really want to be there for it. But I still took the time to joke about toy planes with Birdy just now. Best not to look too closely at that.

"Why didn't you like him?"

It's taking real effort to keep the car steady in this wind, and the visibility is shit. But Birdy's less tense than she was before we stopped, when her hands were clenched in tight balls on her lap, so I keep talking. "Would you believe he was pretending to be a shitty boyfriend to teach her overbearing family a lesson?"

She snorts. "No way. That's rom-com nonsense."

"And yet." I squint and lean forward in my seat, wondering if my brights might help with visibility. They don't.

"For real?" She practically squeals it, and I'm thrilled to hear the animation in her voice. "Oh, that's fun. I'm an only child, so sibling interactions are fascinating. My dissertation actually deals with birth order and communication patterns in familial relationships marked with abandonment."

"Your dissertation?" I'm sure my surprise isn't flattering, but shit, I'm surprised.

"Oh, did you think you scored with the hot bartender chick last night? Sorry, no." She gives my leg a jokey pat. "You took home an overstressed grad student who only moonlights as a hot bartender chick."

I shuffle through the bits that I know about her, but none of them add up to a full picture. "So the University of Wisconsin-Milwaukee?"

"Yep. Sociology PhD."

"Yet you bartend in Vermont." This girl has me begging for whatever scraps of personal information she's willing to part with, but as expected, she's not forthcoming.

"Also yes."

"Do you want to get a job as a professor?"

"Maybe someday." She shrugs restlessly. "Right now, I don't want anything tying me down. No obligations other than finishing my degree and figuring out where to go next. Travel to Sri Lanka? Take improv classes? Who knows!"

Her bravado sounds forced. I wait for her to say more, to explain what's so terrible about a life with structure and someone who relies on you, but she falls silent again.

"So how'd you—"

"Look out!" she cries.

Her shout sharpens my focus, and I slam on my brakes, narrowly avoiding the red brake lights stretching in front of us. The traffic jam hadn't been visible until we were almost on top of it, and my heart's in my throat as we skid to a stop mere inches away from the bumper of the car in front of us.

I hit the hazards and glance in the rearview mirror to confirm that the cars behind us have safely stopped too, and then I let my head fall forward onto the steering wheel, pulse racing.

"What does the weather report say now?" I ask without looking up. "Is it supposed to let up anytime soon?"

Birdy grabs her phone and pokes at the screen with a shaky finger. "Shit."

"That's a no?"

"Continuing snow and wind gusts worsening through 4 a.m., when the snow finally lets up," she reports.

That means hours more of dangerous travel, and if the traffic around us is any indication, we're not likely to make much progress.

"Shit." I run my hands through my hair as I think through the logistics. It's the 21st. If the snow clears up tomorrow, the rest of the trip's doable in one long shot across Pennsylvania, Ohio, and Indiana to get to my parents' place in enough time to take the kids sledding on the 23rd as I promised. Of course, if it doesn't clear up, I'll be screwed.

Well. Better screwed than stuck in the middle of an interstate pile-up.

"What's the next town down the road?" I ask.

She squints at her phone screen, the brake lights in front of us painting her face a lurid red. "Three more miles to Buffalo, and then there's Niagara Falls."

"Okay." I scrub my hands down my cheeks and inch the car forward. "Let's hope we can find a hotel."

Chapter 7

Birdy

I'm perched on a stiff hotel chair when the lock clicks and Sebastian enters with our luggage.

"I didn't know what you needed, so I grabbed…"

His eyes widen as he takes in the rest of the room.

"I already called and asked," I say in as even a tone as I can manage. "They apologize that it's not two queens like we requested, and no, they don't have any rooms they can switch us to."

Sebastian's eyes travel from me to the king-size bed and back.

"Um. Okay. Should we—"

"We should be adults about it and just try to get some sleep." Sure, the thought of lying next to him all night makes my skin tingle, but it's nothing I can't ignore.

Sebastian, meanwhile, looks horrified. He hasn't set the bags down yet, and his throat works as he swallows, eyes back on the bed. It sends the embarrassment I thought I'd banished earlier in the day spiking through my veins.

"I'm not going to maul you or anything." I cross my arms over my chest and lift my chin. "Or do you want to try our luck at another hotel?"

He slowly shakes his head, exhaustion hanging off of him. Last night wasn't the most restful for me, and I'm guessing he didn't fare much better. Plus, he just drove for hours in shitty conditions. He needs to sleep.

"No. This is fine." He sets the bags down. "Do you want to change first?" He jerks a thumb to the bathroom, and I nod and grab my suitcase, grateful to escape so I don't have to watch him process how close we're going to be all night long.

Once I've washed my face, brushed my teeth, and changed into my sleep shirt and shorts, I ease the door open to find that Sebastian's now wearing flannel pants and a dark tee.

He looks good, the bastard. But his obvious reluctance to share a bed makes it clear where his thoughts are, which is just as well. A repeat of last night would be an absolute disaster in so very many ways.

He takes a little travel kit with him into the bathroom, and when he steps back out, I've already slid under the covers.

"I'll sleep on the floor so you—"

"Nope." I was ready for this, and I'm shutting it down. "You need the sleep. On a mattress."

His eyes trace up the comforter to where I'm covered to my chest. "You're right." But his eyes roll to the ceiling as he sucks in a deep breath. "We're adults."

He exhales hard and returns his travel kit to his suitcase, and as he does, he jostles my canvas bag, which flips over to reveal a gaudy pink boa.

"Oh, sorry." He moves to set it upright, but pauses and opens it wider. "Is this Miss Gouda?"

I'm tired. I'm stressed out from our almost accident. I'm turned inside out by hours in the car with Sebastian. And I definitely, absolutely do not want to discuss why I'm hauling that drag queen ostrich halfway across the country. And while the sight of Sebastian St. Claire brandishing Gouda's glittery magnificence is hilarious in the abstract, the whole situation also reminds me that I'll never truly be able to leave Burlington behind. So at the risk of another emotional breakdown, I limit my response to, "It is."

He turns to look at Gouda like she's the third member of this conversation. "Why do you—"

"Just"—I close my eyes and pinch the bridge of my nose to hold back the tears—"just leave it alone, okay?"

He stills, then sets her carefully down on top of the bag. "Okay." A beat, then, "I still think she needs a tiara."

Oh, how I wish I could giggle along to that. I wish I could be that girl from the bar again, but I don't have the bar anymore. I don't know if I'm that girl anymore.

He finishes getting ready in silence, and by the time he slides into bed, all my thoughts disappear except for *this man is going to sleep next to me tonight*. He's sticking to his side as carefully as I'm sticking to mine, and things are awkward again. Not the tense hostility from this morning, but I'm distinctly aware that I've seen Sebastian naked, and before things ended poorly, they were incredible. The reminder has me pressing my thighs tightly together.

"Lights off?" His gruff voice doesn't help my skin forget his touch.

"Yes please," I say quickly. We both click off the lamps on either side of the bed, plunging the room into darkness. For a while, the only sounds are from the hallway outside, where a door slams and someone with a heavy tread makes their way to the ice machine.

Almost without meaning to, I whisper, "I've always wanted to visit Niagara Falls."

I don't know why I'm keeping my voice down, but it feels right to murmur confessions into the blackness surrounding us.

"Oh yeah? Why's that?"

I shrug, then realize he can't see it.

"I don't know. We didn't take a lot of vacations growing up, and Niagara Falls always looked fun and touristy. Stay in a really cheesy hotel with, like, a heart-shaped bed and satin sheets. Take a boat out to see the falls up close. Get soaked with spray." I roll to my side and curl my knees into my chest.

I realize how that might sound and add, "I'm not asking us to stop obviously, and they probably don't even make hotel rooms like that anymore. I'm just..."

What *am* I just? I'm just sharing inane confidences with a stranger.

A kind stranger who laughs softly on the mattress next to me. "Well it'd be a terrible time to be on the water what with the blizzard."

"Ha. Yeah." I sigh. "It was a stupid thought."

"No." His answer's immediate, and the mattress dips as he rolls to face me. I can barely make out his profile in the tiny bit of light trickling under the room door. I can see the outline of his jaw, the fall of his hair. "It's one of your dream vacation spots. It'd be weird for you to be so close without thinking about visiting."

His kindness has me blinking back tears, and I absolutely clamp down on that shit. I cannot cry in front of this man again. But I didn't expect him to be so understanding about it.

Then he shocks me.

"If things were different..." He starts the thought but doesn't finish it, and every cell in my body strains in his direction to find out how he was going to finish that sentence. If things were different... what, exactly? If the weather were different, he'd have made time to stop? If our night together hadn't ended so badly, he'd have looked for a hotel with red satin sheets?

It's ridiculous to even fantasize about that, especially because Sebastian seems like someone I could fall for, and he's come into my life exactly when I've sworn off anything deeper than "you smell nice, let's do this."

He doesn't speak again, just exhales softly in the dark, and it sounds so sad that even though I don't want to risk uncovering more things about him to like, I ask, "How was today supposed to go for you?" This topic is safer than the what-ifs that hang between us.

There's a soft chuckle in the dark. "Not at all like this." The blankets slide across my skin as he shifts positions on the mattress. "My dad was going to pick me up from the airport even though we all know I could just grab a Lyft. My mom would've been baking all day, so the whole house will smell like butter and chocolate and cinnamon."

"Your folks live in Chicago?" I try to keep my voice casual, but I wouldn't be asking if I wasn't interested.

"Oak Brook," he says. "They still live in the house where my sisters and I grew up."

"That's sweet." I sound almost wistful, which is ridiculous; the big-family thing has never been my style. Then again, family dynamics are what I'm studying, so I might as well use Sebastian as a convenient case study. God knows he's talkative enough to be a whole chapter of my dissertation.

Yep. It's academic curiosity and nothing more that has me asking, "So do you live nearby?"

"Nah, Detroit," he says. "But I always come home for Christmas. It's a huge deal for my parents. They both love it. They singlehandedly keep the garland-and-twinkle-light industry alive." We breathe together in the dark for a bit before he says, "It's almost embarrassing how magical it all was when I was a kid. We all went to pick out a tree together. Every room got decorated. Mom has a whole book of recipes that she only makes at Christmas, and we'd look forward to it all year."

"Like what?" What Sebastian's describing is so foreign to me. Our holiday spirit was extended as far as the bar, and that's where it stayed. But

Sebastian's family had rooms full of decorations and December-only recipes? It's hard to imagine.

"God, so many things. Homemade salami. Oatmeal fudge bars. Roll-out cookies that took a full day to decorate. Two types of punch." He laughs softly. "Green for kids, and red for adults because it's got vodka. Let me tell ya, the year I turned 21 and got to try red punch for the first time? That was a big year."

"Awww, my big boy with his red punch," I joke, then immediately want to strike the words from the record. Sebastian St. Claire cannot be *my* anything.

He doesn't acknowledge my weirdness, although he shifts closer. "We do a huge Christmas Eve dinner that everybody pitches in to help cook. And then it's just a free-for-all after that. The kids stay up late and try to guess what's in each present and the adults drink spiked hot chocolate, and there's music and some kind of holiday movie in the background. Then on Christmas, it's pajamas all day and tearing through presents and eating all the sugar-based foods."

"That all sounds..." I don't know how to answer. *Different* feels like an insult, but it is. I grew up with zero traditions. Actually, that's not true; Lizzie's Tap stayed open over Christmas, so my holidays were mostly spent wiping tables and running dirty glasses to the dishwasher. So yeah, the childhood he's describing couldn't be more different than mine, and although I've never spent much time wanting what other people have, the reverence in his voice as he talks about it fills me with a restless longing. I am who I am because of my childhood, so there's no point wondering who I'd be if I'd spent my Christmas mornings surrounded by wrapping paper shreds and cookie crumbs.

These thoughts have me so unmoored that I blurt out the other thing that's been buzzing around my brain all day.

"Do you know what's crazy?"

His quiet laugh tickles my ears. "Is it driving halfway across the country in a blizzard with a stranger?"

"Nah, that's just a Tuesday for me." I'm aiming for breezy when in truth I'm still bothered by what went down in Stilton Grove. The way I almost stayed even though every part of me was screaming to get the hell out. "What's crazy is ol' pervy Pete back at the rental place. I didn't even look that cute!"

"What do you mean?" I can practically hear the frown in his voice.

"I mean," I say, starting to wish we were still talking about Sebastian's perfect childhood and not my own neuroses, "that I wasn't exactly at peak hotness today. I don't know why that guy would work so hard to get me on his office couch."

An almost-growl rumbles through his chest. "You and I both know that guys like that don't really care about looks." I can't see his expression, but his tone is dark, and the back of my neck prickles at the thought of it. God, what did that man say while I was at the car that has Sebastian sounding so primal and protective?

The anxious buzz I've been dealing with since Lizzie's death bursts to life in my brain, reminding me that nobody's around to care what happens to me anymore. But before I can spin out, Sebastian says, "Anyway, I disagree.

You looked hot as fuck today." There's a beat, and then he says gruffly, "Good night, Birdy."

With that, he falls silent, and I listen for a long time as his breathing evens out.

He may be able to fall right to sleep, but his words set my nerves on fire, and now I'm aware of every place where the sheets brush against my overheated skin.

You looked hot as fuck today.

Who drops something like that and just rolls over and conks out?

My road trip partner, that's who. And I need to do the same because tomorrow's going to be another long travel day. I don't know if this conversation just made it harder or easier to sit inches away from him for hours and hours.

It's my last thought before exhaustion from the day claims me.

Chapter 8

Sebastian

"I'm changing it," Birdy announces as I howl in disapproval.

"No way! That's only song number four."

She just bats my hand away from the dial and spins it until she finds a rock station. "See? Isn't that better?"

I grumble at her and try to hide my grin.

I should be having a miserable time. The weather's still utter shit. We finally made it through New York State only to hit a traffic snarl in Erie, Pennsylvania, and now we're detouring from I-90, which takes us deeper into Ohio and adds an hour to our trip on top of the already slow pace from the snow-packed roads and occasional wind gusts. My back and shoulders are on fire from the stressful driving I've been doing, and since we didn't add Birdy to the rental agreement as an additional driver back at the airport, she's technically stuck being a passenger only.

But all things considered, I'm having a great time. Something about sleeping next to each other has thawed the ice between us, even if we did stay on our separate sides of the mattress all night long.

"I can't believe you nixed 'Feliz Navidad,'" I say, shaking my head sadly.

"'Feliz Navidad' is the worst Christmas song known to man." She juts out her cute little chin, and I risk taking my hand off the wheel again to point an accusatory finger at her.

"First, 'Wonderful Christmastime' is the worst Christmas song known to man," I tell her. "And second, this means you only get four of your pop drivel before I get to turn it back, not five."

She crosses her arm over her chest as I change the terms of our radio-sharing agreement. "I can't believe I ended up in a car with a Christmas guy on December 22nd." Then she leans forward to peer out the window, her brow furrowed. "Is it my imagination or are the roads getting bad again?"

Although she hasn't outright said anything, Birdy's a bit of a nervous traveler.

"Nah." I slant her my cockiest smile. "Don't worry, I'm a professional."

She purses her lips. "You're only a professional in the air, captain."

Fuck, I shouldn't love it when she calls me *captain*, but I do. And now I'm wishing she'd known about my title two nights ago because something tells me she absolutely would've called me that in bed.

Wait, nope. Bad. Thinking about that night is the wrong move.

Yet what do I do next? I growl out, "I do just fine on land too, thanks," and she blushes.

All of a sudden, it's like someone threw a switch inside the car and ignited an electric current between us. This is the insane chemistry I felt at Lizzie's Tap. This is why I agreed to take her back to my hotel. In that moment at the bar, Birdy wasn't a stranger. She was the other half of me that I recognized from across the distance. And her pretty blush now is warming a place in my chest that's been empty for a long, long time.

I can almost see the sparks crackling between us, and I want to cling to it, want to keep this livewire current between us alive. And I'm almost certain she's thinking about our night together too because she dives into the snack bag at her feet and pulls out an orange. "Citrus break?"

Her voice is maniacally chipper, and she's clearly trying to change the subject. But I don't fight it. This line of conversation isn't going to lead anywhere; we're just getting to the outskirts of Akron, which means if things go smoothly from here, I can drop her at the train station in a little over six hours, and I'll be at my parents' in time for eggnog and Hallmark movies. She and I will never see each other again.

The thought causes a weird little swoop in my stomach, and when she says, "Hand," I obediently turn my palm up so she can deposit a pile of orange slices into it. She insists on peeling them for me so I'm not distracted while I'm driving, as if her pressing fruit into my hand with her deft fingers isn't distracting enough.

I chew a few slices before I say, "Christmas guy. You called me that before. What is that exactly? Because the way you say it, it doesn't sound like a compliment."

She gives a musical little laugh. "Oh, you know. A *Christmas* guy. Decorates the weekend after Halloween. Wishes he could listen to the music year-round. Owns unironic holiday sweaters." She wrinkles her nose at the thought. It's adorable, so I play along.

"Hmm. Well I limit myself to December for the music, and my sweater collection's magnificent." I scratch the back of my neck and notice the way her eyes follow the curve of my biceps while I do. Thank you, short sleeves and high core-body temp. "But I don't really decorate my apartment since I spend Christmas with my folks."

"So Detroit? Why there?" she asks.

I shouldn't be flattered that she remembers where I live.

"It's a junior base for my airline, so that's where I started, and I never bothered to move." At her confused look, I explain, "It's easier for new pilots to get positions at junior bases. But I'm senior enough now that I could request a transfer."

"So why not move to Chicago? Or did you put down roots in Michigan?"

She's turned in her seat to face me, and while I can't really take my eyes off the slippery roads, I can feel the weight of her gaze on me.

"I like Detroit. My neighborhood, my apartment, my friend group." I tap my thumbs on the wheel as I get my thoughts in order. "But yeah, I would like to move closer to my family someday. I always thought..." The rest of it's a little too revealing, but her patient silence makes me finish the thought. "I guess I always thought I'd move back home when I settled down and got married."

"You're planning to woo a Michigander to Illinois?"

"Well. I've never found anyone worth persuading. And believe me, I've looked."

"Aww, the Christmas guy wants to find his Christmas girl."

She pats my hand in mock sympathy, but I give her a truthful answer. "I really do. She's just been hard to find."

Watching Darby fall for Gabe made me picture my own future, and I didn't like the thought of being the only single St. Claire sibling at the next family Christmas. So I spent the past year on the apps, getting matched up by friends, the whole nine. And here I am heading home for the holiday as the only single St. Claire sibling.

"Lots of first dates?" It's like Birdy's reading my mind, or maybe that's just my bleak expression.

I sigh. "So, so many."

"See, the trick to that?" She leans close like she's about to impart some big secret and faux-whispers, "Just don't date. Then they can't let you down."

She leans back again with a flourish of jazz hands, and although I laugh at her theatrics, it brings me down a little. I haven't been able to shake the thought that, despite the ups and downs, Birdy's the kind of girl I'd want to bring home to my family.

"So that's why you've still got an apartment in Detroit with no Christmas tree in it," she concludes.

"Correct." A semi roars by us in the left lane, driving way too fast for the conditions and leaving our little Chevy shaking in its wake. I grip the steering wheel to keep it under control and risk asking her a personal question in return. "What about you? Is there a tree waiting for you in Milwaukee?"

I can practically see her walls going up. "No." Again, she doesn't offer any more details, but this time, I feel comfortable pressing a little bit more.

"So you're not a Christmas girl?"

She stares intently out the windshield rather than looking my way. "It just wasn't a big deal when I was growing up."

"Come on," I scoff. "What about at the bar, with the bow and all?" I feel a little stupid obsessing over her green Christmas headband, but she'd looked like an adorable gift to me from the universe in it.

"Tips, darling. Tips," she drawls. "It worked on you."

"Oh, that wasn't the bow." I practically growl it and am rewarded with more pink in her cheeks. But she doesn't elaborate, and her silence lets me gather up all the facts about herself that she's dropped. I pop another orange slice into my mouth as I consider what I know.

"You always shut the hell up about your family," I say, "but what I've been able to put together is that you grew up not taking a lot of vacations or celebrating Christmas, and now you're in grad school in Wisconsin, but you have a bag with the ostrich mascot from a bar that's halfway across the country."

Her shoulders tense as I speak, but I've already shared my story. I need hers.

"I don't quite know what to make of all of that, but I'm kind of dying to know," I say. "What's your deal, Elizabeth Denton?"

She doesn't speak, just zips and unzips the top few inches of her bright red coat over and over. She's not wearing her hat at the moment, and her blond hair curls around her cheek, begging to be touched.

She sucks in a huge breath. "So the thing is, I was—"

Then a rock hits our windshield with a crack like a gunshot. All hell breaks loose.

Chapter 9

Birdy

I start screaming the instant the road disappears behind a dense web of cracks.

Sebastian doesn't join me in shrieking his head off, but he does switch into action-hero mode as he coolly decelerates, flips on the hazards, signals to move onto the shoulder, and brings us to a stop out of the flow of traffic. This despite the snow-packed roads and still-gusting winds buffeting us.

Once we've come to a rest, he exhales shakily and asks, "You okay?"

"No! We almost died!" My heart's thundering, and I'm sure my eyes are Disney-character sized in fright.

Sebastian reaches over to wrap his hand around the back of my neck, and I flinch. "Hey. We're fine."

"I know!" I shout, then slump against his shoulder. "But that sucked."

"I know." He exhales hard, his nerves showing for the first time as he strokes his thumb along my jaw.

"God, I'm an idiot," I mutter, dropping my face into my hands. "I'm sorry."

He releases me to give my shoulder a brisk squeeze. "It's okay. It was scary."

"What happened?" I lean forward to touch the windshield, which is a mess of cracks and splinters right down the middle

"A rock hit us. And for it to be this bad, there must've been an existing crack or something." His jaw clenches. "Fucking rental company."

He looks frustrated enough to shatter himself, so I make myself useful and open the glove box.

"What are you doing?"

I grab the rental paperwork. "This isn't drivable, right?"

"No." He gives a tight shake of his head. "Not all the way to Chicago."

"Right," I say as briskly as I can. "So I'm calling customer service to see what we need to do." Maybe if I make myself incredibly useful, it'll wipe away all the screaming I just did.

But twenty minutes later, neither of us is happy.

"Tomorrow at 2? That's the earliest you've got?"

Although Sebastian's tone is authoritative, it doesn't magically change the appointments the guy on the other end of the line already has scheduled, and Sebastian snaps that he'll call back to confirm our location for the repair and stabs the END button with a strangled groan. When the rental company told us to replace the windshield and send them the bill, we didn't count on there being only one repair place that services this stretch of Ohio or that most of their staff would be out for the holidays.

"Goddammit," Sebastian grits out before letting his head fall back against the seat.

As frustrated as I am by what's clearly going to be a pain-in-the-ass delay, I can't imagine how upset he must be. I'm going back home to my houseplants. He has nieces and a nephew counting on him.

Besides, we both know what needs to happen now. There are no other rental cars available nearby. There's no way to safely travel any reasonable distance with this windshield. There's nothing to do but wait until tomorrow afternoon.

Sebastian rolls his head to look at me, defeat in the sag of his shoulders. "How close did you say the next town is?"

"The exit's in twelve miles."

With a sigh, he fires up the engine and pulls into traffic. I don't know how he manages to see through the web of cracks to get us safely to the exit, but he does, craning his neck to catch slivers of unobstructed view as we travel.

He laughs in disbelief when the road sign with the name of the town pops into view.

"Bermuda? For real?"

"For real," I reply. "Let's hope we don't disappear forever."

"I wouldn't count on it," he grumbles as we exit the interstate.

At least there's two beds this time.

"Which do you want?" I ask.

Sebastian responds by rolling his suitcase to the one closest to the door. "In case someone tries to break in," he explains, and I can't help but laugh.

"What, you'll wake up from a dead sleep to confront the intruder and keep me safe?"

I wrinkle my nose at him, and he frowns back. "Yeah, exactly. I'm sleeping between you and the door."

I set my own suitcase on the bed closest to the window. Miss Gouda stayed in the car this time.

"You do know how threatening that sounds, right? Like to me?" I unzip my bag and flip it open, rooting around for my travel kit, where I'm hoping I packed some painkillers. After screaming like the final girl in a horror movie, I feel a headache coming on.

When there's silence from the other side of the room, I glance over my shoulder to see Sebastian standing rigid at the foot of the bed, fingers of both hands spread wide.

"Birdy, I—"

"Oh my God, I was kidding." I find the bottle and pour two aspirin into my palm. "You're my travel buddy. I trust you."

If anything, his jaw clamps even tighter. "Your travel buddy."

I pat his chest on the way to the bathroom to get some water. "Yes. My travel buddy."

It's a reminder to myself as much as it is to him, and when I emerge from the bathroom, he hasn't really moved. God, he must be pissed about yet another delay. At least I know how to give him some space.

"I'm going to shut my eyes for a bit. Try to shake this headache." I flip the covers of my bed back, grateful I pulled on leggings this morning. If I was in jeans, I'd be wondering how weird it would be to take them off before climbing between the sheets.

This shakes him out of his trance. "Headache?" He takes a step toward me. "Can I do anything?"

I shake my head, then wince. "No, thanks. But maybe we could find some dinner once I've napped?"

"Yeah, of course." He picks up his phone and turns toward the door. "I need to call the windshield place to confirm our location for tomorrow and then let my family know it'll be another day."

"Wait, you don't have to—"

But he's already out the door before I can tell him that I don't hate the thought of falling asleep to the rumble of his voice. I drop a pillow over my head and ponder whether I'm on a road trip with the last genuinely thoughtful guy in America. How many other men would've yakkity-yakked away from the bed next to mine while I tried to sleep? Probably all of them.

When I wake up, the light in the room is low, and Sebastian's propped against his headboard, one ankle crossed over the other, an iPad in his hands.

"Feel better?" he asks once I'm upright.

"Blarg," is all I can manage as I bat my tangled hair out of my eyes. "Headache's gone, at least."

"Excellent." He sets the tablet on the bed next to him, and I wriggle around to face him.

"How'd your family take the news?"

"Insultingly well." He links his hands behind his head. "Apparently they can decorate sugar cookies just fine without me."

"Heathens." I yawn and stretch, then grip my growling stomach. My headache's gone, and I'm starving. "Food time?"

"Food time," he agrees. "I figure we can head to the lobby and ask the clerk if there's anything close by."

"Good idea." Or it was until I glance down at myself. "Can you give me, like, ten minutes to clean up?"

He cocks his head and takes in all my rumpled, travel-stained glory. "Whatever you need. Take your time."

How does he look so good after two days on the road? His soft-looking sweater stretches over his broad shoulders, and his jeans aren't creased and baggy like mine get after sitting in them all day.

He's a warlock, I'm sure of it. And that's on my mind as I wheel my whole damn suitcase into the bathroom and flip on the shower. He said to take my time? I'll be taking *alllll* the damn time.

Thirty-five minutes later, I'm scrubbed, toweled off, blow-dried, curled, made-up, and looking as cute as possible in my least travel-gross jeans and the cream cable-knit sweater that looks like I stole it from one of Chris Evans' douchier characters. I even scrounged up a pair of earrings from the bottom of my makeup bag.

Sebastian shoots to his feet when I finally exit the bathroom.

"Wow. You look… wow."

I give a little twirl. "No road grime here."

He ruffles his hair as he stares at me, for a moment looking as frazzled as he did during the worst of the blizzard the night before. Then he smooths the silky brown strands back into place and grabs my coat off the chair where I flung it, holding it out so I can slide it on. I try not to sound breathless as I thank him, but it's hard when he runs his hands over my shoulders before letting me go to reach for his own coat.

We're quiet as we walk to the elevator and head to the lobby, where the rail-thin clerk with the huge mustache greets us. "Are you off to the beach?"

This stops us in our tracks.

"Come again?" Sebastian asks.

The clerk gestures toward the main entrance. "The festival." At our continued blank looks, he says, "The Christmas in Bermuda festival? I assumed it's why you're in town."

A slow, delighted smile spreads across Sebastian's face. "A Christmas festival, you say?"

I groan theatrically. "Are you kidding me?"

"No," the confused clerk says. "It's the 46th annual event."

"And it's, what, got craft booths and hot chocolate vendors and more decorated Christmas trees than you can shake a candy cane at?" I ask flatly.

He nods eagerly. "You bet. And don't miss Sandy Claus."

"*Sandy Claus*?" I mouth at Sebastian, who bounces a little in excitement. He actually bounces. This adorable Christmas dork.

The clerk's still raving about the festival. "The township sells holiday-print Bermuda shorts that you can wear over your winter clothes, although the really hardcore fans just wear the shorts."

I snort at the same time Sebastian guffaws.

"Excellent," he says, glancing at me. "Whaddya say?"

"How far away is it?" I ask the clerk. "We don't have a functional car."

He points out the window. "There's a sleigh that gives rides to and from the festival. It should be coming down the main drag in the next twenty minutes or so."

"A sleigh!" Sebastian looks happier than he has since that night at Lizzie's, and with a little flutter of my belly, I realize that I'm going to agree to whatever he wants if it keeps him smiling at me the way he did that night: a little flirty, a little sexy, a lot charming.

"Lead the way," I say with a sigh, pretending to be put out about it. But deep down, I'm weirdly excited as he puts a hand on the small of my back to usher me outside to wait for our Bermuda Christmas carriage.

Chapter 10

Sebastian

"This is awesome!"

I'm shouting to be heard above the wind rushing past us in the back of the sleigh, but Birdy cups her hand around her ear and pretends she didn't hear me.

"Sorry, it's hard to catch what you're saying over how ridiculous this is!" she shouts back.

I can't help myself. I sling my arm along the back of her seat and lean close. "No grinching allowed," I warn, trying to keep my face stern. But her eyes are dancing with laughter as she leans into my side, and I can't help but grin right back.

Because she's right. This is ridiculous. We're riding in a red and green dune buggy being pulled by a horse with a starfish-and-holly festooned garland draped around its neck and a driver in a tropical-print shirt over his green-and-gold elf costume.

"Here we are, folks!" says the man from the driver's seat as the horse clip-clops to a halt in front of a tiny town square that looks like someone's beach-themed man cave exploded all over a quaint Christmas village. All the action takes place at the booths and tents lining the four streets surrounding the town square with a postage stamp-sized courthouse dropped in the middle. Real Christmas trees stand next to inflatable palm trees, and they're all draped with bright white twinkle lights. Festival-goers dressed in beachy pastels rub elbows with people in bright-red Santa hats. Christmas music blares over speakers set at various intervals around the square, but the version of "Jingle Bells" that's playing is backed by island-appropriate kettle drums.

"What in the tropical fever-dream mashup hell is happening here?" Birdy murmurs after I've taken her hand and helped her down from the buggy.

A red-cheeked, white-haired couple strolls past us holding coconuts with straws sticking out of them.

"I don't know," I murmur back, "but I think that's frozen hot chocolate they're drinking."

"God, please tell me there's an option to add vodka."

"Let's find out."

We merge into the crowd to get the lay of the land. The clerk wasn't kidding; everywhere we look, people are strolling in candy cane-striped Bermuda shorts. And lots of them are, indeed, braving the winter weather in their bare legs.

"Excuse me," Birdy says to a pair of college boys walking past with their knees exposed to the wind. "Where can we buy some of these shorts?"

Their enthusiastic directions to a vendor a few booths down make me think there's vodka around here somewhere after all. But I don't get a chance to ask; Birdy grabs my hand and tows me toward the shorts booth.

"Looking forward to showing off those legs?" I ask her.

"Oh, these aren't for me, captain," she says with a wicked gleam in her eyes before she turns to the vendor, a weather-beaten man sporting a stubby gray ponytail. "Hi! My friend wants the full Christmas in Bermuda experience. Can you outfit him with your finest holiday shorts?"

The vendor studies me carefully. "Over the jeans or full festival?" he asks.

"Full festival," Birdy answers, glancing at me with laughter on her face. "You're tough. You can handle it." She pats my chest, and if this is what it takes to keep her smiling at me like that, I'll wear the damn shorts all night.

The man reaches into the stack of merchandise and holds up a pair. "Waist 31?" At my impressed nod, he gestures to a tiny tent behind him. "Change in there."

I do as instructed, swapping my jeans for candy-cane shorts that almost hit my knees. I'm sure they look ridiculous with my lace-up cordovan boots, but Birdy's delighted laugh when I emerge from the tent makes it worth it.

"No, no, I insist," she says, reaching for her purse and extracting a credit card that she hands to the vendor, who gives her a receipt and a bag to stash my jeans in. "Now where can we grab some dinner?"

Just like the college boys, the vendor's thrilled to direct us to a booth a few stops down that's selling meat pies, codfish cakes, and small game hens on sticks, along with roasted chestnuts, hot wassail, and Bermuda banana ice cream. It all smells incredible, so we buy a little bit of everything and trade bites back and forth as we wander through the booths.

"Ever been to a German Christmas market?" I ask before slapping my forehead. "Oh wait, of course you haven't."

"Of course I haven't!" she confirms with a laugh. "Is it like this?"

"God no." Then I stop at a table full of hand-carved nutcrackers and wooden Santa Clauses. "Actually, a little. The one in Chicago is like this but forty times bigger. You'd hate it."

She wanders ahead of me and runs her finger gently over a blown glass ornament in the shape of a dancing bear. "Maybe." The next ornament that catches her eye is an ostrich that looks a little like Miss Gouda in its red and green ruffled skirt and gold high heels. She holds it up and peers at it in wonder.

"You should get it," I tell her.

She frowns and sets it right back down. "No tree, remember?"

She pulls me to the next booth, displaying brightly painted home decor signs with sayings like Santa Crossing Only and Happy Ho-Ho-Holidays. My mom would love them.

"How you doing there, Christmas Boy?" Birdy asks when a gust of wind scours the street and sets the light-wrapped inflatable palm trees dancing. "Willing to admit that you're freezing your sugar plums off?"

"My sugar plums are fine," I say with as much dignity as I can. Yes, it's fucking arctic out, but I kind of love it. The other festival-goers who opted to go full festival give me knowing nods as they walk past, and the glow of this weird little community's keeping me warm.

Well that and Birdy by my side, looking adorable in her red parka and pompon hat. She can claim to hate this all she wants, but her smile's brighter than the lights wrapped around the fake palm trees as she sips hot chocolate from a coconut. Her joy is almost enough to banish the sting of being relegated to travel buddy status earlier today. I may have gone from the guy who gave her an orgasm so strong it uncorked her emotions bottle to her platonic car friend, but at least I'm showing her a good time.

Another gust of wind blasts down the street, and I wince. Yet again, my lack of foresight in packing a hat and gloves is biting me in the ass. Cold knees I can handle. Cold ears fucking suck.

Without warning, the kettle drum carols overhead fall silent, and the brassy sounds of a marching band kick up. Within moments, row after row of high schoolers in black and gold uniforms come parading past, playing a loud rendition of "Rockin' Around the Christmas Tree" that's semi-on key and performed with such enthusiasm that it's hard to mind. Birdy bops along to the song as they turn the corner, the music distorting a little in the night air as they vanish from view.

Unfortunately, holding still during the performance made the cold worse, and I try to sneakily reach up to rub my ears with my freezing fingers.

"Sebastian!" Birdy clucks her tongue and grabs my hands in her mittened ones, rubbing them briskly. "What are the odds that somebody around here is selling hats?"

The odds turn out to be very good. When we turn onto the third street surrounding the town square, we run into a table full of hand-knit items made by the mother and daughter who own the yarn shop one town over and are excited to help me pick the right winter gear.

"Not that one, Mom," the daughter says, shaking her head at the black hat the older woman's holding. "He needs something brighter. Blue, maybe?"

"That one." Birdy points at one toward the back of the booth. "It'll bring out the green in his eyes."

The grandmother leans over the table to peer closely at me. "You're absolutely right, sweetie. There is a little green in all that brown."

She reaches for the hat Birdy indicated, leaving me staring at my travel buddy in surprise.

"What?" she asks almost defensively. "I told you I think you have pretty eyes."

Why this matter-of-fact statement unleashes a warm feeling in my chest, I have no idea. God, is this all it takes to jostle my emotions bottle loose? Birdy noticing a tiny detail like that about me?

"Here you go!" Yarn mom presents me with a bright green hat. "Try it on."

I do and instinctively turn to Birdy for her approval. She cocks her head, squints, and reaches up to make a tiny adjustment to how it sits on my head. Then a smile spreads across her face, and I wonder what she's seeing on mine. Attraction? Affection? Lust? Because I'm feeling all of those things right now.

"It's perfect," she says, then asks, "Do you have matching mittens?"

They do, and when we stroll away after a round of thanks, my knees are still exposed, but I'm miles warmer. The only downside is that there's no reason for Birdy to take me by the hand anymore.

Kettle drum Christmas gets louder as we turn onto the final street, where we're greeted by a truly indescribable sight: Santa Claus in full beard, hat, red velvet coat, and Bermuda shorts. He's sitting on a green beach chair in the middle of a sea of sand, and the garland overhead is the same mix of holly and starfish that the dune buggy horse was sporting.

"I know him," Birdy breathes, and before I can bust her for quoting from *Elf*, she pulls us into the line to meet the man of the hour.

"You know," I say as we move into place behind two women and their three small children, "for somebody who doesn't like Christmas, you're really getting into this."

"Oh, shut it," she says, bumping her shoulder against mine. "This turned out to be fun."

"It really did." I'm supposed to be at my parents' right now listening to my dad complain about how the neighbors botched their Christmas light display and offering praise as my mom showed off her latest quilt creation. Instead, I'm in line to meet Sandy Claus with a woman whose name I didn't know forty-eight hours ago. And I'm good with it. Loving it, even. Whatever sadness has plagued Birdy over the past few days isn't anywhere in her clear blue eyes right now, and I hope I had a little something to do with that.

My initial impression of her in the bar wasn't the right one, but neither was my second one. She's playful and smart and surprising, but she's also a little guarded, a little wounded. Thank God I stuck around long enough to see all these different shades for myself. It makes me wonder if I wrote off other women too quickly when I went looking for someone to get serious about.

Then again, maybe none of those other women worked out because the right woman was waiting for me at a bar in Burlington, Vermont.

But no. That's not what's happening here. Not with my *travel buddy*.

As we inch closer to the front of the line, I lean down to whisper, "You have sat on Santa's lap before, right?"

She rolls her eyes. "I may be Christmas-averse, but I'm not an alien."

"Hate to break it to you, but you look downright Christmas-curious right now," I tell her. Somewhere along the way, she switched from frozen hot chocolate to the hot stuff, which comes with a candy cane sticking out the top. At my pointed glance, she takes a big swig of it and smacks her lips.

"You're just jealous because you already finished boring old eggnog," she says, although she doesn't protest when I swipe her hot chocolate, take a sip, and hand it back. She smiles and takes a swig herself, putting her lips on the same spot I just drank from. Was that intentional?

It's not a question to ponder when she's about to sit on Sandy Claus' lap, so I force my thoughts away.

"Actually, my mom makes the world's best hot chocolate. Nothing else compares," I tell her. "So there's no point trying anybody else's."

For a split-second, I worry that I've just painted myself as some kind of weird mama's boy—or worse, a Christmas mama's boy. But Birdy's face softens. "That's really sweet."

Before I can answer, the pastel-clad assistant calls us forward, and we walk across the sand for a little truth-telling with the jolly old elf.

"Ho ho ho!" Santa chortles as Birdy tentatively settles on his lap while I opt to stand on his other side. "Naughty or nice this year?"

She shoots me a laughing glance. "What do you think, captain?"

"Definitely a little bit of both," I tell Santa, whose beard is the real deal and who shoots me a wink before nodding his head at Birdy, setting the bells on his hat jingling.

"Sandy Claus approves," he says. "And what do you want for Christmas, little lady?"

Birdy's mouth opens, but nothing comes out, and that sadness I thought was gone comes rushing back, clouding her expression. But she blinks it away and says tartly, "A pony."

Santa nods somberly. "I'll see what I can do. And you, young man?"

What do I want? This night to never end. Birdy not to think of me as a temporary friend. The search for my person to be over. How startling to think that those three things might very well be intertwined.

But I don't say any of that. Instead, I dig the toe of my boot into the sand and tell Santa, "World peace."

Chapter 11

Birdy

If you'd asked me how I expected to spend the evening of December 22, I'd never have guessed it would be helping a ridiculously sexy commercial airline pilot carefully unload four nutcrackers from a horse-drawn dune buggy in the middle of nowhere, Ohio.

"The kids are gonna flip," he says as we set them on the hotel room dresser next to the TV. Each wooden figure has a different robe, beard, and facial expression, and Sebastian took his time picking the perfect one for each of his sister's children, forking over a small fortune for them. "It's their first Christmas heirlooms."

He says it without a trace of irony. Then again, if those kids have even a trace of the St. Claire Christmas DNA that I've observed, I fully believe they'll be displaying these nutcrackers in their nursing homes eighty years from now.

Once he's given each of the nutcrackers a final once-over, he says, "I need to get into a hot shower. Try to get some feeling back into my legs."

He gestures, and what can I do but look down to confirm that he does indeed have legs? Nice legs. Legs I'd hate to see fall victim to frostbite.

I bid a fond silent farewell to those goofy shorts as he shuts the door behind him, and I try not to imagine him peeling them off as the shower starts up. By the time he's emerged from the bathroom in a cloud of steam, all flushed and scrubbed clean, I've changed into my pajamas and can slip past him to brush my teeth and wash my face.

When I'm done, I find Sebastian standing next to his bed, contorting his back with a grimace.

"What's up?"

"Nothing." He rolls his shoulders. "Just some stiffness from all that time in the car."

"Ah." A beat. "Would you like a back rub?"

His eyes travel over my thin shorts and T-shirt. I resist the urge to cross my arms over my chest and hope my nipples are behaving.

"I shouldn't." His gaze catches on my mouth before pulling up to my eyes.

"It's the least I can do since you're chauffeuring me cross country." I try to make the offer sound light and friendly, but my voice is an invitation. Oops.

He swallows hard. "Okay. Yes, that would be incredible."

I cross the short distance to his bed and murmur, "On the bed. Face the wall."

His eyes flash with heat, but he obeys, settling cross-legged with his back to me so I can climb onto the mattress to kneel behind him. I only hesitate for a split second before I settle my fingers on his neck, and he gives a half-groan, half-sigh when I press into the muscles there. I tell myself it's relief from the soreness and nothing else.

He's lucky that Lizzie's one indulgence was massages; I learned early on what feels good and what doesn't when it comes to muscle manipulation.

"You're so tense," I say as I work.

His shoulders shift under my hands as he shrugs. "Flying's a lot less stressful than driving through a blizzard."

"I really am grateful, if I haven't said it enough." I shift my pressure downward. "Even though you stole my car."

"It was never your car." He shoots me a smile over his shoulder, and warmth settles over me knowing that it's an in-joke between us now and not an argument. I work his knotted muscles in silence for a bit, and before long, I'm lifting off his shirt so I can really dig into his back. His broad, well-muscled back.

He eventually ends up stretched out on his stomach with me straddling his ass as I stroke him with long, firm movements. My shorts are too short for this; my thighs are pressed into his sides, and the friction against my core as I work is starting to make my nipples *really* misbehave.

"What were you going to ask Santa for, really?"

My hands still at his question, which chases away all the delicious heat that was building between my legs.

"Just..." I run my hands down the muscles on either side of his spine. "Connection, I guess."

"With other people?" He lifts his upper body to look at me, and I roll off of him and settle onto the mattress so we're facing each other.

"Yes. No." Why did I even say that? I'm trying to *avoid* relationships right now. But he's patiently waiting for a better answer, so I take a moment to consider how much I want to share before speaking again.

"I wouldn't say I have trust issues, but at the same time, I don't have many people in my life that I'm truly close to." There's not enough distance between us on this bed for what I'm about to say but I take a deep breath and start talking anyway. "For me, the main person was my grandma. She raised me. I'm named after her."

Understanding dawns on his handsome features. "Lizzie's Tap."

I nod and hope I can get through this without another round of earth-shaking tears. "She owned it. I grew up there. Started helping out as soon as I was able to see over the bar. My whole life, it was the two of us until I left for grad school."

"Your mom?"

"Split when I was little. Last I heard, she's in Arizona. I don't really know, and I don't really care." It took a long time for that to be true, but it is now. She never gave a second thought about me, and thanks to therapy and years of absence, I'm finally able to return the favor.

His calm, steady gaze warms me as I try to tie together all the little pieces of my life.

"Lizzie wasn't a big fan of Christmas. Or vacations. Or relationships. She threw everything into running the bar and didn't have much time left over for anything else. But she taught me to stand up for myself and go after what I want. She taught me that it's better to be on your own than go chasing after someone who's just going to disappoint you. She was…" I shake my head, unsure how to put my stern, proud grandmother into words. "She was so tough."

I'm painting a harsh picture of Lizzie, so I add, "But she was also incredibly fun. Just such a weird sense of humor. She's the one who put Miss Gouda up on the bar and added to her outfit over the years."

"She did a great job with that." His brows draw together for this next bit. "So she's…"

He already knows the answer I'm going to give, but he asks it anyway. I appreciate that clarity amid the wave of grief.

"She died in March. She left the bar to me." I roll to my back and say this next part to the ceiling. "I hadn't seen her in almost three months. Too busy at grad school to get back home over spring break."

Sebastian starts to reach for me, then pulls back. "I'm so sorry, Birdy."

"Thanks. It sucks." I twist my head, and his eyes are practically liquid in the low light of the room, all sadness and understanding. "The estate finally settled out last month, and I had to decide what to do with it. Lizzie told me I could sell it or keep it, whatever would give me the life I wanted. So I was in Burlington this weekend to sell it."

The agony of that decision is still sharp. I decided to say goodbye to the life we shared, but I did it to open myself up to something new.

"That night we met was my final night bartending there. I stopped by the next morning to grab Miss Gouda, then I went to the title company to sign the paperwork. After that, it was straight to the airport. The rest you know."

After a moment, he nods. "Well that explains the crying."

I groan and bury my face in my hands, grateful for the lightness in his tone. "I'm really sorry I freaked you out." My voice emerges muffled through my fingers. "I just couldn't bring myself to sleep at Lizzie's that night. It didn't smell like her anymore after all those years of it being home. It made me so sad. And then you came along."

I turn to smile at him, but his face has gone slack.

"Oh." He blinks. "I see." After a beat, he sits up and grabs his phone from the foot of the bed, where he left it. "It's getting late," he says, eyes on the screen. "We should get some sleep."

"Sure," I say hesitantly. "It was a long day."

I climb off his bed, feeling awkward as hell about the abrupt end of our conversation, but Sebastian just crawls under the covers and rolls so his back is to me, leaving me to turn off the room lights.

I do, saving the lamp between our beds for last as I slide between my sheets. They're cold without Sebastian's big body to warm them.

"Good night," I say quietly as I click off the lamp and plunge the room into darkness.

He doesn't respond, although a few seconds later, his voice floats through the darkness. "I'm sorry about your grandmother."

"Thanks," I say in a scratchy voice

What the hell? There's no way I can fall asleep like this, not after I had my hands all over his body and then he shut me out. But a quick replay of our conversation gives me a strong inkling of what went wrong.

"Hey. Captain," I say into the dark. "Did I hurt your feelings?"

"No."

His answer's so terse it's almost funny. I sit up and flip the lamp back on. "Sebastian," I say in a light reprimand.

He sits up too, scowling in the light. "So any guy would've done?"

His mouth's set in such a sulky line that I have to laugh. "Is *that* what you took from all of that?"

Instead of answering, his jaw tightens, and he crosses his arms over his chest.

"Just so we're clear," I say, "I wasn't planning to go home with *anyone* that night. I was going to suck it up and spend one last night at Lizzie's until you wandered into my bar."

The corners of his lips tighten. "Lucky me."

"Lucky *me*," I shoot back, irritated enough that I don't bother hiding the truth of that night from him. "You had this, I dunno, this *glow* that I couldn't stop looking at, and every time you caught my eye, it was like something in here vibrated, like a gong strike." I press a fist between my breasts. "So yeah, I decided to see if you were feeling it too, and yeah, I hoped it would keep me from feeling so alone for a little bit. Because Sebastian?" He's looking at me now, really looking, and I unload it all. "You have your family. You have your mom and your dad and your sisters and their husbands and their kids. You have *everything*. And I had Lizzie. But I don't have her anymore, and that makes me all alone in the world. And I'm fine with that. Losing her was terrible, and I never want to go through something like that again. But you were *with* me that night, and I wanted to hang onto that feeling for a little longer. That night, it was either going to be you or nobody, okay?"

By the time I finish speaking, I'm actually breathing a little hard, but all Sebastian's doing is looking at me blankly. Christ, will I never stop humiliating myself in front of this man? When he doesn't respond, I huff and reach for the light again. "Fine. You and your hurt feelings can go to sleep. I'll just—"

"I felt it too." He scrubs a hand through his hair, leaving it adorably ruffled. "I felt it too, but for a second it sounded like you were just looking for an easy lay. It made me feel..." He shrugs in irritation.

"Oh no." I soften my voice to be gently teasing. "Did I make you feel like a piece of meat?"

"Yeah. A little." His cheeks redden. It's the cutest.

Cautiously, I leave my bed and cross back to his. "Grade-A pilot meat." My smile widens, and the tightness in my stomach eases when he grins sheepishly back.

"I'm sorry the goods let you down," he says.

I perch on the edge of his bed, and his eyes drop to my mouth when I wet my lips. "The goods were great," I say softly. "I just had some things to work through."

"And now?" His voice is equally quiet, as if he's holding his breath waiting for my answer.

"And now..."

I could cross the last few inches between us and kiss him right now. He'd let me. I know he'd let me. And then he'd *devour* me. I see it in the flush riding high on his cheekbones, in the rise and fall of his chest as he sucks in a shallow breath. He felt that gong in his chest too, and he wants it back just as much as I do.

But the last time we reached for that together, it unraveled me, and I can't risk that again. Not when our time together's about to end. He needs to get home to his family, and I need to move on with the rest of my life. This was an odd, beautiful little interlude, but it's going to end. It *has* to end.

And that's why I pull away. It's a tiny movement, but it breaks the spell, and I watch Sebastian blink to clear away the lust that had been building between us.

I draw in a shaky breath. "And now we both need to sleep."

"We both need to sleep," he agrees. If he's disappointed, it doesn't show.

I switch off the lamp for the second time, but I'm too cozy to move, so I slide down until my head rests on his pillow. He joins me, and his hand finds mine, his fingers tracing the contours of my palm.

"Did you wish you were with your family today?" I whisper it into the dark, unaccountably nervous to hear his answer.

"No." He sounds a little surprised to realize it. "There's nobody else I would've wanted to spend today with."

The confession settles inside my chest and makes me wish I'd leaned forward to kiss him. That I was in a place to explore a relationship with someone real and solid and good.

Within a few minutes, he's breathing deeply, obviously asleep.

I should go back to my bed. But I don't want to leave this little pocket of warmth here next to him. The darkness wraps around me, pinning me in place, and his fingers are still entwined with mine as I lose myself to sleep.

Chapter 12

Sebastian

I wake up wrapped in Birdy.

Her cheek presses into my chest, and since I never did put my shirt back on, it means her breath fans across my skin with every soft exhalation. She's worked her foot between my ankles, and although I try not to disturb her as my brain slowly comes back online, I must shift accidentally because she murmurs and burrows more tightly against me.

"What time is it?" she grumbles sleepily into my armpit.

"Don't know." I let my hand trace down her side. God, that's a thin shirt covering her curves. "Doesn't really matter since we can't do anything until the windshield guy gets here."

"Mmpf." I recognize the instant she wakes up enough to realize our positions. Her whole body stills until she calmly starts to disentangle herself from me. I don't want to let her go, but I do.

"Wow." Her smile's almost shy. "And we did such a good job of staying on our own sides in the last hotel."

"It's because I looked so good in those shorts, isn't it?"

She laughs softly and rolls out of bed, padding to the bathroom. When she emerges, she walks straight to her luggage and starts to paw around. "Damn, are all my sweatshirts in my other bag?" She rubs her hands up and down her arms.

"I have a spare in my suitcase. Help yourself."

She flashes me a smile and flips open the top of my bag, shifting through my neatly packed clothes. I clearly didn't think this through because she has to shift aside a pair of my boxer briefs before she finds my old Cubs sweatshirt. She pulls it over her head, and I definitely catch her holding the collar to her nose to give it a quick sniff before tugging the hem down. It hits below her shorts, but that still leaves plenty of leg. When she goes to flip the lip of my suitcase closed again, she tilts her head.

"Um. What's this?"

I don't know if she thinks I should be embarrassed to see her holding up the green bow headband she was wearing at the bar, but I'm not, not really.

"You left it behind." I stretch and swing to sit on the edge of the bed as she looks incredulously at the object in her hand.

"No, the point is, you kept it?"

I shrug. "It was proof that I didn't make you up."

She bites her lip, spinning the headband between two fingertips.

"Yeah, I really was there and gone, wasn't I?"

"It was more of a come-and-go situation," I say with a smirk. This gets a groan and a laugh out of her, as I was hoping.

"Take it back," I say. "I know you want to. We turned you into a full-blown Christmas girl yesterday, me and Sandy Claus."

Her laugh is light and happy, and it chases away the last of the awkwardness that came from waking up in each other's arms.

"I don't know, it matches your new hat." But she tucks it away in her suitcase, and I'm glad. I held on to that little scrap of green to prove that I hadn't made up that beautiful, charismatic girl who let loose in bed and then ran without a backward glance, but I'm delighted that she wants to keep it. Maybe it'll remind her of me someday when she looks at it in her Christmas tree-less apartment.

The reminder that this is our last day together is a sobering one, and it gets me up and out of bed. I should be annoyed by yet another delay, but all I really want to do is find a diner that serves a really good breakfast so we can linger over coffee and I can pull more confessions from Birdy's pretty pink lips. I want to see her nose crinkle when she laughs. Get her to tease me some more about my soft-boy Christmas tendencies.

So that's what we do. We spend the hours until our repair appointment at the little restaurant down the block, talking and laughing and arguing about movies and politics and dream vacation spots. We go through the camera rolls on each other's phones, describing the highlights of our lives to the other person. We're both full of pancakes and slightly burned coffee by the time the mobile repair van pulls into the hotel parking lot, and then we set off on the final leg of our trip.

The tension starts to creep back in the closer we get to Chicago.

The final leg of our journey has been uneventful, especially compared to the past two days, and it passes quickly despite my efforts to hold on to the last of the time I have with her.

I drive the speed limit. I make sure we stop for bathroom breaks. I regularly resupply our snacks. But the sun sets, the sky turns black, and my stomach gets more and more leaden as the traffic on I-90 starts to pick up as we near Chicago.

"Seriously, you don't need to go," I say. "You're welcome at my parents' house for Christmas."

I've extended this invitation three times now. I'm probably starting to sound a little desperate, but it's intolerable, the idea of Birdy getting on the train at Union Station that'll take her to Milwaukee, where she'll spend Christmas alone. She just confessed how isolated she feels, but she's refusing to even consider a holiday surrounded by conversation and music and lights and food and laughter and love. Everybody deserves that, but especially her. I saw the way she lit up as we walked along the streets of Bermuda. I heard the longing in her voice when she was finally honest with me in the hotel room. She craves that joy; she just doesn't know how to reach for it.

Like now. She lifts her stubborn little chin and says, "I told you, I'm not going to intrude on your family's Christmas."

"It's not intruding."

"Easy for you to say. You're not the stranger in this scenario."

I bite back a growl. It's the same response she's given me twice before. "You're not a stranger to me."

She rolls her eyes. "How old am I? Where did I go to undergrad? What am I allergic to?" When I don't answer, she says, "We're basically strangers."

Every part of me wants to tell her that she's wrong. If you count up the hours, I've spent more time with her than the last half dozen women I've dated. I told her serious things and silly things, and I've seen her laugh and cry and yes, I've seen her body shake as she comes. She's not a stranger. She didn't even feel like a stranger the first time we spoke.

I thought she felt that way too, but here she is, intent on getting away from me yet again. It's that first day on the road all over again. I hate it, but after this time with her, I understand it. She lost the only person she loved, and she's putting up boundaries to avoid future pain.

Once again, I have to adjust my idea of her. She's the girl from the bar and the airport and the hotel that first night. She's the girl putting on a brave face for Sandy Claus, the girl with no family, the girl who whispers her secrets in the dark. She's all of those things, and underneath it all, she's scared.

I want to tell her it's okay, that I can handle her fear. I can be brave for both of us. But she's made it clear that all she wants is for me to drop her at the train station and drive away.

Fine. I can do that.

"What time did you say your train leaves?" I ask tightly.

"9:15."

I glance at the clock. It's 8:20 p.m. "Cutting it close."

She taps her fingers on her knee. "I know. But if the traffic is good, I'll be fine."

"Because traffic is always so reliable in downtown Chicago." I sound like a dick, but I'm fucking frustrated, and I want her to know it.

She exhales. "If I miss it, there's another train at 11:30."

Great. She would rather hang around Union Station until midnight than come home with me. Message received.

My offhanded comment turns out to be prophetic, and we hit thicker-than-normal traffic heading into Chicago that slows us to a crawl. This part of the interstate is always congested, but on December 23, it's basically bumper to bumper.

"Shit," Birdy says a nervous eye on the clock.

"If you miss this one, do you want me to at least stay with you while you wait?" I hate myself a little for asking, but I'd also hate myself for not asking.

She just shakes her head tiredly. "Stop. I'm not a passenger on your airplane or a piece of luggage that you have to deliver. You've dragged me around with you long enough."

"Fine." I push down my frustration. "If that's what you want."

"That's what I want."

She's being practical. I know that. We want different things, and prolonging this will just make things harder.

But my stomach's still in knots as we drive in silence. Once we reach our exit, I take it and maneuver through the congested city streets as quickly as I can. God forbid I'm the reason she's late for the train that'll take her out of my life forever.

We pull up in front of Union Station, that massive stone building in the heart of Chicago, and I bring the car to a stop in the drop-off area. It's busy, of course, but at this time of night it's not nearly the zoo I expected. I open my door and walk to the trunk, pulling Birdy's luggage out over her protests that she could do it herself.

"I fucking know you can do it," I snap. "Just let me help this one last time."

She bites her lip but stops arguing, and once she's slung the bags over her shoulder and gripped her suitcase, she hesitates. I don't know what's going through her mind, and I wish she'd hug me or kiss me or, hell, punch me. These have been some of the most stressful, surreal, and meaningful days of my life, and I don't know what to do now they've come to an end.

"Thanks." She gives me another one of those sad smiles. "You were really great." Then she turns and walks off between the big stone columns.

And just like that, she's gone.

Numbly I slide into the driver's seat, but I don't put the car into gear. Instead, I rest my wrists on the steering wheel and let myself drift. I need to return it to the rental place. I need to let my family know I'm on my way home. I need to forget this whole interlude happened.

But I can't seem to make myself pull away from the spot where I saw her ponytail swish out of sight as she was swallowed by the entrance to the building. I'm almost tempted to abandon the car and run in after her, force my phone number into her hands. But for God's sake, the woman's already turned me down three times.

She doesn't know my family. She doesn't know how delighted my mother would be to have another person to fuss over for Christmas. How much shit my sisters would give me about bringing home a girl, but how over the moon they'd be at the same time. I can't be surprised that Birdy, with her solitary upbringing, would be skeptical of that welcome. And maybe that's what makes us fundamentally incompatible.

Swallowing the bitter tinge of disappointment, I signal and prepare to pull away from the curb. But a red parka catches my eye as I glance in the rearview mirror.

It's Birdy, back on the street with her luggage, frowning down at her phone.

I roll down my passenger-side window. "What the hell, Birdy?"

Her head snaps up, her face slack with surprise. For a second, it looks like she's going to bolt, but she shifts her bag higher up on her shoulder and walks over, bending to speak through the window. "What are you still doing here?"

I don't have a good answer, so I shoot back, "What are *you* still doing here?"

She blows out a tired breath. "I missed the 9:15, and it turns out there is no 11:30. That's only on Fridays."

"And you weren't going to come find me?" Then a new, worse thought occurs to me. "Wait, did you actually know and were just trying to get rid of me?"

"No! And it's not like I had your number or anything." She worries her lower lip between her teeth, which makes me think there's more going on in that complicated little head of hers.

I sigh as I reach across her empty seat to flip open the door. "Get in. I'll take you to my parents' house for the night, and we can come back in the morning."

Her mouth hardens. "I already told you, I'm not going to be the random girl you picked up at a bar who crashes the St. Claire family Christmas. I'm just going to go to a nearby hotel. The first train tomorrow leaves at 6:10, so I won't even be there that long."

God, she's stubborn.

"Well I'm not leaving you on the street after dark. Get in." She hesitates because of course she does, and I grit out, "I swear, I'll drive you to a hotel, and then you'll never see me again."

She hesitates again before finally nodding, and I pop the trunk so she can stash her stuff one more time. When she slides into the passenger seat, I try to ignore how right it feels to have her there, like she's brought a burst of crisp, clean air in with her.

As we drive away from Union Station, I offer one point of clarification.

"By the way, you're not a random girl I picked up at a bar," I say. When she looks at me in confusion, I add, "We both know that *you* picked *me* up."

Chapter 13

Birdy

The last thing I wanted was Sebastian walking me to my hotel room.

That's because it's the *only* thing I wanted.

Saying no to his invitations, telling him we had no future, shutting down the hope I saw in his eyes, it almost killed me. But it was also the right thing to do. Nice-guy, nice-family, nice-job Sebastian St. Claire is the real deal, and I'm not in the market for real deals. Didn't I just sell the last thing in the world that was truly mine to avoid having roots?

Sebastian St. Claire feels like roots.

And now he's dumping my suitcases inside the door of the hotel room he insisted on walking me to, and I let him because I'm weak. The door swings shut behind him, and God help me because I don't know how I'll push him out now.

"Thanks for letting me carry your bags," he says, looking around as if he's a security expert who can tell at a glance if the window locks are secure. Then he crosses to the nightstand and picks up the pad of paper set there.

"What are you doing?"

He grabs a pen, scrawls a few lines, and rips off the top paper.

"This is my cell phone number and my parents' address. If you change your mind, please call me. Or just show up." His eyes are soft, exactly the way I like them. "I promise you, every member of my family would be thrilled if you did."

He folds the paper and slips it into the front pocket of the bag holding Miss Gouda, then shakes his head as if he can't believe the situation he's found himself in.

"I think I have to be done here, Birdy. Have a nice life."

He gives me one last searching look before turning toward the door.

"Wait!"

The word bursts from my throat, and my brain and my heart go to war over what to do next.

My heart wins.

I cross the room in three short steps, and when I reach him, I throw my arms around his neck and press my lips to his.

He freezes for a terrifying, stomach-churning moment, and I'm sure he's going to push me away.

Instead, he groans and buries his hands in my hair, angling my head up so he can meet my lips with his own. "Oh thank Christ," he murmurs as he backs me toward the bed.

I don't answer because I'm too busy pushing his coat off his shoulders and sliding my hands under his shirt to pull it up and off. Then we're kissing again.

"Are you sure?" He pulls away to sweep his thumbs over my cheeks. "Because you spent the whole day trying to get rid of me."

"This is the only thing I've been able to think about all day," I breathe.

"You've got a funny way of showing it," he says, but he's lifting my shirt over my head and turning his attention to the zipper of my jeans.

"I wanted this last night," I tell him as I kick off my shoes so I can pull my jeans all the way off. Then I undo his button and zipper and reach inside to close my fingers around his cock, which is as excitingly hard as I remember.

"Oh my God," he groans, and after a little more tugging and hopping, he's naked and I'm naked, and we're stretched out on the bed I was supposed to sleep in alone tonight. He reaches for me, but I duck away to press kisses into his chest, his stomach, his hip. He groans even louder when I suck on the skin under his belly button before finally moving to his cock, where I circle my tongue around the head before sucking him all the way into my mouth.

"Oh *God*." His hands sink into my hair as I move along his shaft and dig my fingers into the straining muscles of his thighs. "I wanted your mouth on me last night," he grunts out.

"I wanted that too," I say thickly, trading my lips for my fingers. I wrap my fist around him and use my saliva to jack him slowly, loving the way his hips lift with each pass of my hands.

"I also wanted this." He wraps his hands around my hips and helps me inch up his body until I'm positioned over his mouth. "Grab the headboard."

It's the only warning I get before he pulls me down onto his face and his tongue glides through my pussy.

"Fuck," I hiss, scrambling for purchase on the headboard as he starts to lick me, spearing his tongue into my cunt before sliding it up to my clit, over and over until I'm panting and my thighs shake. "That feels so good, captain."

As the nickname falls from my lips, he growls against my core. "Call me that again."

"Captain!" I cry as he keeps that growl going, bringing a whole new series of vibrations into the mix. The tension builds between my legs as I work myself over Sebastian's eager mouth, back and forth, chasing that pleasure. As my movements get more frantic, he lets go of my hips and splays one hand on my lower back while he palms a breast with his other hand. The scrape of his skin against my nipple sends me over the edge, and I come in a rush, tensing and shuddering against his lips.

I tumble sideways off of him afterward, and he uses the new position to suck my other breast into his mouth until my spine curves off the mattress.

"Sebastian," I whimper, my hands stroking down his back. "Captain. Condom, now."

But he ignores me, takes his time kissing his way up my neck and over my jaw to claim my mouth with his. "Not until you come again."

"No, I—" But his fingers are already in my pussy, spreading my wetness over my still-sensitive clit, and I forget what I was objecting to. "Yes," I pant, raising my head to watch what he's doing to my body. "More of that."

He thumbs my clit and spears me with his middle finger, pumping and circling as his teeth catch my nipple causing a sharp burst of pain that explodes into pleasure a few seconds later. The second orgasm hits me even faster than the first one, and his breath is hot on my breast as I shake under his fingers.

"Good girl," he whispers as I come down. "My good girl."

He pulls away to find his discarded jeans, and then it's wallet, condom, ripped package, all handled so quickly that his body's covering mine again before I can even start to miss it. Only then does he slow down to hold my gaze as he slides into me, inch by hot, hard inch. I shudder once he's fully seated, my inner walls still sensitive and fluttery, and he pulls out slowly before driving himself back in with a quick stroke, using the motion to capture my lips with his. His tongue invades my mouth, his cock fills my pussy, and I'm nothing but sensations. The friction, the sting of his teeth on my earlobe, his breath hot against my cheek.

"So good, so good," I croon, not sure if I'm agreeing with his assessment of me or telling him how good he is in return. His approving groan tells me it's working for him whichever way he's taking it.

I dig my fingers into his ass so I can pull him even tighter against me. The sharp press of my nails makes him groan, interrupts his rhythm, and his breathing saws in and out of his lungs as his hips snap forward once, twice. On the third stroke, he cries out my name and empties himself into me, collapsing with a groan. Once his breath normalizes, he wraps his hand around the back of my neck and kisses me over and over, tongue sweeping against mine possessively. But eventually his kisses gentle, and he pulls away with a final brush against my lips.

"How's your emotions bottle?" He brushes his thumb down my cheek as if he's checking for tears, but my eyes are dry.

"Intact," I say. "And full of happy stuff." My body still tingles from two incredible orgasms, and I'm coming down from that high all wrapped up in him. We're still going our separate ways tomorrow, but tonight he gave me a new memory to replace the old one. I'll cherish it, even if saying so out loud makes me feel too vulnerable.

After we clean up, we curl around each other in bed, only waking up to use the second condom Sebastian has stashed in his wallet. It's slow this time, and I'm on top, hands resting on his chest as I work myself up and down on his cock while his bright, pretty eyes lock on mine. I see it on his face, the way he's taking this in and making himself remember. I see the things he keeps himself from saying after he makes me come and my pussy squeezes an orgasm out of him right back.

We're both on the edge of sleep when he finally gives in.

"Come home with me," he says. "Not so you won't be alone for Christmas, but because I want you there. I want you there with *me*."

My heart thumps with longing, then just as quickly freezes because I *can't* want that. He's asking me to experience all the big, bright family things I've missed over the years. It'll draw me deeper into his life, the kind of life I'm running away from.

It takes me a long time to answer.

"I can't. This is just"—I wave my hand through the air, frustrated with him, frustrated with myself—"this is a few stolen days. It was fun, but it's all too fast. Too soon. None of this is real."

I almost want him to come up with an argument that proves me wrong, some sweet words to convince me that you can be this sure about someone else after only a few days. But his only response is to hold me tighter and press his lips against the top of my head.

"Okay," he whispers. "Okay."

And that's why I sneak out of bed at 5 a.m. while he's still dead to the world. I dress in the dark, gather my luggage, and slip out of the room, holding my breath as I wait for the elevator and not releasing it until I'm through the lobby and out the door into the pre-dawn darkness to make the three-block trek to Union Station.

Sebastian's sleepy post-orgasm smile is too hard to resist, so I'm doing the thing I know I need to do.

It still sucks though.

At the ticket counter, I frown at the Christmas greenery on the wall, which looks naked without sand dollars attached to it. But I buy my ticket and board my train, and if I have to dash away a tear as it pulls away from the station, who's there to see it but me?

Chapter 14

Sebastian

"Are you ready to tell me what's wrong with you?"

Darby's exasperated words cut through the noise of the Christkindlmarket, which is swarming with last-minute shoppers on Christmas Eve. When I tried to sneak out of the house for this errand, Darby caught me, and somehow we ended up volunteering to take Celeste and Aaron's kids with us. So now I'm on a potentially doomed mission with my sister, nieces, and nephew along for the ride.

"What makes you think something's wrong with me?" I snap.

Darby gives me a wordless *That, for one thing* look, and I scowl at her and keep the whole group moving toward the tent I'm here to find.

"Everything's fine."

"Oh really?"

I have to slow to let her and the kids catch up. "Yes, really."

"Because you showed up this morning grumpy as hell a full three days after we expected you, and you've barely explained what held you up."

"Blizzard," I say shortly.

"Like I believe that."

The curse of growing up with a sibling only a year older than you is that they know you inside and out and can call you on your shit. But I don't want to let my perceptive sister in on the pain I felt when I woke up to an empty bed this morning.

Of course Birdy was gone. I should've known she would be. Our sex last night had been beyond anything I'd experienced before. Sex with someone I care about. Someone I *know* despite our short acquaintance. And she felt it too. I know she did. I saw her face as she was coming down from that high with me. She was luminous in a way I hadn't seen before. She was happy. With me.

And that's what sent her running out the door.

I wish I could be pissed about her cowardice, but instead I'm at the German Christmas market in downtown Chicago to buy her a gift.

"Is it because of Gabe still?"

Darby's mostly teasing with that. Her boyfriend and I got past our rocky start last Christmas. We're bros now. He even pulled me aside after lunch to show me the ring he's giving to Darby tomorrow morning. I was so excited, I hugged the man.

"We're fine." I signal for the group to stop when I see the tent I'm looking for. "Troops! I need your help."

The children assemble, their mouths and hands full of the giant pretzels we bought them to ensure their cooperation. Their eyes go wide as they take in the rows upon rows of colorful glass ornaments in every shape imaginable: Santas and cats and sleds and croissants and pickles and bears and squids and angels and typewriters.

"I need to find an ostrich ornament. Can you help me do that?"

Darby glances at the four kids, then at the delicate merchandise, and rushes to put her body between them.

"This is a look-but-don't-touch situation," she announces, squatting to get at eye level with the tiny ones. "Can you all search with your eyes only?"

The kids shout their agreement and squirm in excitement, at which point I realize what a mistake we've made.

"Stop!" I bark, and everyone freezes. Ginny's sticky fingers are inches from a display of fragile glass stars, and Kayleigh, Tristan, and Madison have fanned out in front of the jungle animal section. "Let's see who can freeze in this position the longest," I call.

The kids giggle as they lock their limbs into place, and I whisper urgently to Darby, "Can you keep them away from all these breakable things for a few minutes?"

"Not until you tell me why you're looking for an ostrich ornament." Darby crosses her arms over her chest in a stance I recognize as her *I'll die before I back down* pose. I give in with a sigh.

"There's a girl, okay?"

Her face immediately brightens. "I knew it! I told Mom that it had to be—"

"Not a word to Mom." I point at her in warning. "You'll notice the girl isn't here with me. I don't know if she actually wants that, but I'm going to try. And I don't need all that Mom energy directed my way until I figure my shit out."

She gives a wicked laugh and grabs my face in her freakishly strong librarian fingers. "I knew this day would come eventually." Giving my cheeks a squeeze, she baby-talks, "Widdle Sebastian's all growed up!"

"Jesus. Get out of here," I grumble, batting her fingers away.

"Rademacher kiddos! Let's leave Uncle Seb alone and see if we can find Santa!"

The kids shriek in delight and abandon me without a backward glance, which lets me peruse the merchandise without worrying about having to buy the whole shop thanks to grabby little fingers.

For some reason, I'm convinced I need an ostrich ornament. Why, I don't know. I don't have her phone number or her address or anything to go on except the University of Wisconsin-Milwaukee, and it's not like I'm going to mail a gift to her academic department. That would make me worse than the creeps at the bar. Worse than the rental-place guy, even.

So yeah, leaving her the fuck alone is the right call here. But when I spot a fancified blown-glass ostrich in a red tutu with a goddamn tiara, I immediately know that I'm going to buy it. I may never have the chance to give it to her, but that just means I'll have my own reminder that once upon a time, I had something special for a few days in late December.

It's Christmas afternoon, and we're all a little sugar-drunk and weepy.

Gabe proposed to Darby this morning after all the presents had been opened and we were still sprawled around the tree in our pajamas. She cried. My mom cried. My dad cried. Gabe cried. I cried. I'm sure Celeste would've cried too if her kids hadn't been having some kind of crisis in the backyard with their new toys.

After we'd pulled ourselves together following the gift-opening frenzy and emotional rumpus of watching Gabe get down on one knee with a promise to make meatless lasagna for Darby for the rest of their lives, we celebrated with Mom's hot chocolate and a huge tray of cookies she'd baked in the shape of wedding rings and passed off as the ones from *The Twelve Days of Christmas* when Darby asked what was up with all the gold circles.

And now the three women I love the most are gathered in the kitchen debating the merits of various wedding venues and shades of pink while the kids are scream-laughing somewhere upstairs and the men are gathered in the TV room for a football game that none of us cares about. My dad and Aaron are both passed out on the recliners, and Gabe and I are on the couch debating different honeymoon locations.

"I was thinking somewhere in Europe," he says. "Austria is gorgeous."

"Forget Austria. Try Austr*alia*."

"G'day, mate!" he bellows in the worst accent I've ever heard. "Wait, where can you fly us?"

"Boston," I say. "How do you feel about Paul Revere?"

"Meh. How about Hawaii? She's never been to Hawaii. Plus, you know, I get your sister in a bikini."

"Or I hear Alaska is nice," I say brightly.

"Oh, dude!" He slaps his forehead. "I completely forgot to ask. Did you hear about the weird cloud in Alaska a few months ago?"

"I did *not*. Tell me."

One thing my future brother-in-law and I have in common is a love of ridiculous conspiracy theories that we torture Darby with whenever we're together. He pulls up the picture on his phone, and I say, "UFO. Easy."

"That's what they want you to think." He taps the side of his nose. "But it's clearly where they're hiding an escape pod that's taking the chosen few from Earth to the secret moon base."

I pretend to study the picture more closely. "Actually, that's just a gender reveal gone wrong, I think."

"Speaking of," Gabe says, pocketing his phone, "I've got to tell you about Jonesy's latest bachelorette party hijinks."

"I feel like a need a course of antibiotics just to listen to this." Jonesy, first name unknown to me and possibly even to his best friends, is the part-time server, part-time stripper who's working with Gabe to get their landscaping business off the ground. I have yet to meet the guy, but every story I hear about him is more chaotic than the last.

"Nah, nothing like that. But the bride wanted to ride him like a pony, so he agreed because he wanted to give her a send-off she'd never forget, but she slid on the new body oil he was trying out and her earring got caught on the collar he was wearing, and they ended up stuck together until somebody could find a pair of scissors that could cut through leather to set him loose."

Gabe tells the story without stopping for breath, and all I can come up with is, "Wow. So the moral of the story is to carry leather shears?"

"Nah, the moral of the story is that Jonesy needs a nice girl to settle down with so he'll come do landscaping with me full time." He shoots me a speculative glance. "Is the woman you drove home with from around here? Think I could fix them up?"

"Fuck you. No," I growl. So much for my good mood.

"I guess Darby was right," he drawls. "Interesting things *did* happen on your road trip."

I shrug, pretending the question doesn't actually hurt me to answer. "She's not here with me now, is she?"

Just then, the *bing-bong* of the doorbell echoes through the house, and my mom calls, "Could one of you boys grab that?"

Gabe leaps to his feet. "If this were a Hallmark movie, that'd be her here to surprise you."

"We weren't Hallmark appropriate," I mutter, which causes Gabe to shoot me a *Nice job, player* face as he disappears into the front hallway.

A moment later, he shouts, "Hey Seb, is your road trip woman a cute blonde with a green bow in her hair?"

No. Fucking. Way.

Heart pounding, I race to the entryway and skid to a stop when Gabe throws open the door to reveal the woman I haven't been able to stop thinking about.

Chapter 15

Birdy

This seemed like a better idea on the two-hour drive here.

"Hi." I wave awkwardly and search Sebastian's shocked expression for some sign that this isn't the worst mistake I've ever made.

His mouth has been hanging open, and he shuts it with a snap. I still have no idea what he's thinking and wish like hell he'd say something to put me out of my misery.

"You didn't call first," he finally says, and his voice is weird and distant, and I may never recover from the embarrassment of this moment, especially when the good-looking guy who answered the door leans against the adjacent wall with a shit-eating grin.

"Are you gonna invite her in, Seb?"

Sebastian jolts into action. "God, yes. Come in." He grabs my hand and pulls me inside, his eyes fixed on mine and a million questions on his face.

"Hi. I'm Gabe," the other guy says, loping over to me with his hand outstretched. "And you are…"

"*You* are leaving," Sebastian growls, putting his body between me and Gabe, who ambles away with a laugh, leaving us alone. Sebastian's still not saying anything, so I guess it's up to me to go first.

"You broke me," I announce.

His brows meet over the bridge of his nose. "What do you mean?"

I'm sure there are better places to have this conversation than the open foyer of his parents' house, but I can't seem to move from where his gaze has me pinned.

"I mean," I say, "that I got home yesterday and read your note, and I was so glad to have that little scrap of your handwriting. And it occurred to me that the rest of you was *right here*."

"Waiting for you," he agrees, the beginnings of a smile touching his lips.

"And then I looked around and realized that my apartment doesn't have a Christmas tree," I tell him hotly. "I don't even have any hot chocolate mix, and... and I think you turned me into a Christmas girl!" I throw my arms up in disgust.

His sweet smile gets bigger. "Oh yeah?" He steps nearer, and I lower my hands to rest on his shoulders.

"Yeah." My heart's throbbing as I slide my fingers along his neck until they're tangled in his hair. "And it sounded like you were going to be someplace with, like, *extra* hot chocolate. Enough to spare. So I thought maybe—*mmpff*."

He's kissing me. And he tastes so good, so exciting and familiar at the same time that I don't stop, not even when a child's piercing voice says, "Uncle Seb's kissing a girl!"

Eventually I do try to pull away, flustered by the audience we seem to have gathered, but Sebastian murmurs, "Nuh-uh. Not yet," and pulls me tighter against his chest. "I thought you never wanted to see me again, so I need another seco—is that a Rudolph sweatshirt?"

Now he's the one breaking away to glance down at the garish red-nosed creature leaping across my chest.

"Christmas girl!" I jab a thumb at my torso. "See what you did to me? You turned me into me a Christmas girl, and this was all they had left at the truck stop on the way here."

"I love it," he growls, bending his head to kiss me again until a pointed clearing of a throat interrupts us.

"Care to make introductions?" A man who's clearly Sebastian's father is standing in the hallway with the rest of the St. Claire clan flanking him. Sebastian's plump, smiling mother. Two women who look so much like him that they have to be his sisters. The nieces and nephew I heard so much about. The brothers-in-law. All of them grinning like fools as he takes my hand and lifts it to his lips before turning to say, "Everyone, this is Birdy Denton. She's…"

His eyes catch mine, and I can tell he's not sure what to call me. I've been so many things to him since we met: a hookup. An irritant. A travel buddy. A lover. But I know what I want to be, and I think that's what he wants too. So I offer it up to him now as the best gift I have to give.

"I'm his," I say softly, glancing up and praying he's feeling everything I'm feeling right now.

"She's mine," he repeats, sounding a little dazed, and as we stare at each other, we become the only two people in the room—the only two people in the whole universe, maybe. But we snap back to reality when his mother gives a happy little sniffle.

"I knew there was a girl!" She rushes forward and wraps me into one of the best hugs I've ever had, whispering, "Welcome home, sweetheart."

Unexpected tears catch in my throat, but I manage to choke out a thank you. And then the rest of the St. Claires are hugging me, patting my back, leading me into their magical Christmas house to get to know them all.

I glance over my shoulder at Sebastian as I'm pulled away, and his smile is so radiant that it fills me up. I might never be empty again.

It's close to midnight when we're finally alone.

"I can't believe you're actually here." He still sounds a little shocked even though I'm currently tucked into his childhood bed after spending hours and hours with his family.

"I had to try your mom's hot chocolate for myself," I say with a shrug.

"And?" He smooths a piece of hair behind my ear.

"If anything, you undersold it."

He laughs and kisses me. He's been laughing and kissing me all day. I've never been kissed so much in my life. Short, sweet presses of his lips mixed with long, lingering ones that leave me breathless and wanting to strip him bare.

When we come up for air, I say, "I can't believe this is where you grew up."

"What do you mean?" He stretches out on his side and props his head on his fist while I gesture around us.

"I mean it's like out of a movie. The lights everywhere, the billions of Christmas coffee mugs, the decorated trees in every room." I clasp my hands to my chest. "I get it now, why you were so anxious to get home."

"Less anxious the more time I spent with you," he says.

"Well you have very good taste." Then I bolt upright. "Oh! I almost forgot. I got you a present."

I slide out of bed and dart to the suitcase I packed this morning in the hopes that Sebastian would be happy enough to see me that he'd let me stay. I retrieve the small box, slip the green bow headband back on, and clamber back between his sheets to find that he's also holding a wrapped package.

"Me too."

"How did you...?" I'm too surprised to finish the thought. He had no reason to think he'd ever see me again, but he still bought me a gift? I take it from him and tear off the green and gold paper, gasping in delight when it parts to reveal a beautifully gaudy ostrich ornament.

"A mini-Gouda," I breathe as Sebastian smiles proudly.

"She's even wearing a tiara."

I blink a few times to clear the tears caught in my lashes. "Well now we're really going to have to get one for the OG queen." I set the box carefully aside and swing around to straddle him. "Thank you," I whisper against his mouth as his hands wrap around my waist and he pulls me down to grind against his suddenly interested cock.

I break the kiss with a gasp. "Not yet. You've still got yours." I hand him the little box, and he reluctantly pulls his hands away to take it.

When he sees what's inside, he gives a bark of laughter. "Seriously?"

He pulls out the red airplane with *Sebastian* painted on the side.

"For your cockpit," I remind him.

"Mmm. I love it." He sets it on the bedside table, then turns his attention back on me. "And now—"

"You've got something for *my* cockpit?" I waggle my eyebrows at him, and he part-laughs, part-groans.

"C'mere." He wraps a hand around the back of my neck and pulls me down to kiss him. "This time, you're keeping the bow on."

Epilogue

One year later

Birdy

Niagara Falls is incredible in December.

Of course, anywhere with Sebastian is incredible, but my suggestion that we spend our first anniversary retracing the route we took last Christmas was a brilliant one if I do say so myself.

"How did you talk me into this?" He shouts over the roar of the falls, which is covering us in frigid spray as it churns past us.

"You love it!" I shout back.

"I love *you*!" He wraps me in his arms, and I press a kiss against his jaw.

Although he hasn't put in a transfer request yet, Sebastian's spent more of his off days with me in Milwaukee than he has at his place in Detroit, and I spent most of my summer weekends exploring Michigan with him. Once I've finished my doctoral work and landed a job, he'll figure out his next steps, but we're both hoping to land in the Chicago area to be close to his family.

My family now too.

After our stop at the Falls, we're headed back to Bermuda, where Sebastian's threatening to make me join him in going full festival with this year's novelty shorts. After that, it's straight to his parents' house for the rest of our Christmas festivities. I'm excited about every single minute of it.

"Are you ready to hit the hotel?" he asks after our clothes and hair are soaked through with cold, wet spray.

"You mean, am I ready to warm up in our heart-shaped jacuzzi and then sex you up on our satin sheets?" Finding an over-the-top hotel room in the area had turned out to be harder than I thought, but Sebastian pulled it off, and I plan to reward him for his thoughtfulness.

"That's exactly what I mean," he says.

I slip my hand into his. "Lead the way, captain."

Gabe's friend Jonesy stumbles into a Christmas love story of his own—and it's as sexy and unpredictable as he is. Unwrap *My Not-So-Secret Santa* now!

Acknowledgments

Skye Malone, Genevieve Jack, Tanya Melendez, Natalie Martin, Holly Easley, Megan Remmel: You know what you did, and you know I couldn't do it without you.

Also by Sara Whitney

Hot Under The Mistletoe (in Large Print)

My Fake Bad Boyfriend

My Holiday Hookup Road Trip

My Not-So-Secret Santa

Cinnamon Roll Alphas

Tempting Heat

Tempting Taste

Tempting Talk

Tempting Lies

Tempting Fate

Standalone Novellas

Game On

Ghosted

About the Author

Sara Whitney worked as a journalist and film critic before she earned her Ph.D. and entered academia. She divides her time between professoring, authoring, and entertainment reporting, and she almost certainly has an opinion about your favorite TV show.

Sara writes her sexy, sunny romance novels in Illinois, where she's surrounded by books, cats, half-full coffee cups, and practically empty bags of Swedish Fish. Keep up with the latest news by subscribing to Sara's mailing list at **www.SaraWhitney.com/VIP**

9 781953 565228